Songs *from* Ugly

Discovering Chords of Beauty

Heather Ricks

Editing, cover design, and page formatting by
ChristianEditingServices.com.

ISBN 978-0-578-58241-2

Table of Contents

♫

CHAPTER 1

Out of the Author's Journal

Part 1

♫

It's hard to capture the chaos of the world and put it into words. Journaling leaves me feeling vulnerable, perhaps because I'm placing my innermost thoughts under a lock anyone can pick with a coin. Maybe that's why I've never written in a normal manner. My expression of feelings normally ends up looking something like this:

3/13/88
Worthless
Pink Shoes
The fox took a stroll through the supermarket
What's my purpose
[A drawing of a weird face at the bottom, left-hand corner of the page]

Anyone who looks hard enough at my nonsensical word lists, lines of mismatched sentences, and scribbled drawings can catch a glimpse of my struggle. However, anyone sneaking a peek with their little penny would be sorely disappointed if they wanted to find anything to hold against me. Unless, of course, they could charge me with insanity.

Writing has always been my outlet for joy, pain, confusion, and worship. While journals are supposed to hold secrets that can be reopened years later to laugh at forgotten crushes or to make fun of middle school feuds, I freeze at the thought of letting anyone into my world. My thoughts can just disappear and never be held against me. But writing my struggles into existence exposes what I really think about myself, the world, and God. So, instead of exposing myself personally, I use stories to face my insecurities and pain, to ponder the injustices I see around me, and to cry out to God for understanding. In essence, I journal in the world of fiction as my short stories describe my feelings in characters I can control.

The countless hours I spend crafting one sentence or choosing a single word make me a writing coach's worst nightmare. The truth of the matter is I've never cared as much about the story itself as about the journey it takes me on as I try to bleed out every emotion inside me. Through words and characters and themes, I'm able to search for something deeper that grounds me in a world that doesn't make much sense to me. I write and write until I've exhausted my questions. In the end, when an actual story materializes, I'm the one who's changed.

When I began this process of emptying myself into my short stories so long ago, a consistent theme began to take shape. Beauty continually emerged out of the ugly. That doesn't mean I suddenly saw evil as being good. No. That would be an injustice. However, what I discovered was a persistent beauty that flourished despite the ugly. I just had to dig a little deeper to see it. In my analyzing, groveling, dithering, and doubt, beauty is what I was ultimately searching for, and it came out through my writing.

My hurt, wrapped up in lies, came out in agonizing tears as I prayed to God to help me understand why he'd created me the way he had. I wanted to see something beautiful, and I felt as though the world had diluted my senses enough for me to accept a counterfeit concept of something greater. I sensed there was something more, so I clung to that hope until I was able to bring it close enough to be stunned by its magnificence.

To better understand the pulse that breathes life into my stories, you must be given the key to unlock my thoughts. I realize that, due to the previous nonsense that posed as my journal, you may balk at the chance of looking deeper inside me. For that, you'd be justified. However, for those who want to stick around for the ride, I'll take you for a walk in my shoes as I introduce you to the original character from whom my stories began.

What is beauty to a little girl but to wear makeup, dress up, fix up her hair, and have the attention of all the boys? For me, that was the ultimate dream. I subscribed to teen magazines that showed techniques for correctly applying makeup, gave step-by-step instructions on how to tease and spray your hair into a perfectly fanned tower—it was the 1980s—and taught you the coolest clothing trends that were sure to make everyone's jaw drop as you walked by. I would analyze the examples for hours but still fell short of the ideal look by worldly standards.

I looked up the definition of *ugly* on *dictionary.com*. It reads, "very unattractive or unpleasant to look at; offensive to the sense of beauty; displeasing in appearance." That says it all. Without mincing any words, *ugly* is declared repulsive, even to the extent that the sense of beauty is actually offended by it. As harsh as this sounds, that essentially captures how I felt as a teenager, although I'd probably use a euphemism to soften the sting a little. Maybe something along these lines: Beauty turns her head from ugly ever so slightly in dislike. There. That makes me feel a little better. Regardless, I didn't match the world's definition of what beauty was supposed to look like. I'd somehow offended beauty, and I didn't know how to apologize to win back its love.

But I knew ugly. As a scrawny kid with braces, glasses, and a bad home perm, I lived it every day. I was the one being publicly humiliated and laughed at by gym teachers as the awkward example of how not to do things. As I walked down the hallways at school, guys would punch each other's arms, point at me, scream, and run away in disgust. I had my hair pulled, was the brunt of jokes, and was never asked on a date in high school.

All the terrible things I experienced at school weren't even the root of my problem. They just reinforced a lie told to me at home. For years, my grandmother, who lived with my family, verbally abused me. Each day she called me ugly and told me in many different ways that I was no good, that I was unworthy, and that nobody would want me. All these insults came from a church-going woman, beloved by the people in her congregation. No one else, except for my mother, encountered her in quite the same manner as I did.

Words can be the most destructive weapon or the greatest healing tool. We humans tend to dwell on one negative comment over a multitude of compliments given. That fact gives just a tiny picture as to how regular, extended verbal and emotional abuse can be so damaging. With no outward scarring, the abuse is silent. However, the words, honed to be daggers, are shot straight into the soul. They create wounds deep enough to bleed the life right out of someone. The skin, bones, and veins are left to mimic a body, but all that remains is an empty shell. That's how I felt. Like an empty shell.

Because the abuse I endured was such a normal part of my routine, I didn't even realize the layers of its effect until years later. *Ugly* was the identity I came to embrace. I had a relationship with God, but I compartmentalized my faith and wouldn't allow him to touch that innermost part of me that gave me purpose and meaning. Psalm 139:14 says, "I praise you, for I am fearfully and wonderfully made." Out of the 23,145 verses in the Bible, this is the only one I didn't believe for myself. I was told I was a mistake; therefore, by reasonable deduction, I couldn't have been fearfully and wonderfully made. In my mind, my fate had already been sealed by the words and actions of others.

It was because of my misconception of true beauty that I opened my journal and poured out my pain. I created misunderstood characters that nobody wanted. Their characteristics and experiences didn't exactly mirror my own, but the world in which they lived was a concept I understood. I had the freedom to use their brokenness as a way to dig into the ugliness of my feelings and sort out the truth. I wanted to feel worthy and fought to discover my purpose.

Because I allowed myself to be vulnerable through my writing, an amazing thing happened. In its persistent, all-encompassing, life-giving way, beauty pursued me. I allowed myself to be confused and hurt, but no matter how far I ran, I couldn't escape beauty's influence. Its grand design was all around me, although I'm not sure I recognized it at first.

My parents gave me the example of a loving God. Growing up, I watched my mom wake up every morning to be with God. As she read the Bible, I learned the importance of hiding God's Word in my heart. To this day she's still the prayer warrior for my family across the long miles from home. She modeled God's love. I saw my dad demonstrate the same habits, and before he went home to be with the Lord, he encouraged me to write. I could be anything through my stories, all while changing the world. My dad planted the seed of encouragement that helped me later understand my purpose. Through this, I wanted the same true love I saw my parents had and developed my own personal relationship with my heavenly Daddy, who was big enough to allow me to question, cry, and complain while he held me close.

As life continued, God gave me the gift of

a wonderful husband to continue my lessons on beauty. My husband treats me as his God-given treasure. Every day he tells me how wonderful, beautiful, and talented I am. I didn't accept his words at first, because the image of how he saw me was a foreign concept. This caused several battles as I learned to believe and to trust his love. But drip by drip, like an antidote in an IV, his words have helped to flush out the poison in my life.

My relationship with my Creator and the living examples of Christ's love in others is beauty. No matter how ugly I felt, my eyes were opened to something greater, something beyond me and my circumstances. I began to see everything through the lens of God's grace, love, and redemption. This shift in my focus helped transform my perspective of beauty. In turn, my characters reflect that same discovery of God's beautiful characteristics that are all around us, qualities that can often be hidden by the doubts that lock us in a lie.

I now understand Psalm 139:14. Even though I may still have times of self-doubt, I'm learning how fearfully and wonderfully I'm made. God gives every person a purpose no matter who they are and what they have to overcome. I was given a new opportunity for my empty shell to be resuscitated. Despite the former abuse, I no longer have to hang my head in shame, and I can be used for God's glory.

Because many people walk through struggles—many more incomprehensible than my own—I want to open my heart, become vulnerable through my words, and share with you the pages of my journal. They may seem like just a series of fictional stories, but there's more to them than that. Each character reflects a piece of me as I searched for something beautiful. It's my hope that, if you sort through the words, get to know the characters, and listen carefully with your heart, you'll find the same undercurrents of the beauty I discovered as they sing to your soul.

CHAPTER 2

Songs from Ugly

♩

Benny's staring at a weed—a brown, dead, gangly old thing. He crouches his little body over it and scrutinizes his subject. If he knows we're here, he doesn't acknowledge our intrusion in the slightest. The cows graze all around him, ignoring the boy who's been still for so long he's become part of the scene. Even his violin, which rests beside him nearly hidden in a tuft of crabgrass, is left forgotten.

James points in Benny's direction. "Benny's been out in my field for over two hours now just staring at that thing, Ms. Vivian. I left him alone while I worked and kept an eye on him. When I was headed back inside, I tried to get him to move, but he wouldn't have any of it."

James, my neighbor and dear friend, always keeps a close watch over my grandson and me. He never bothers to call unless he deems it necessary. A seven-year-old boy watching a pathetic weed with a violin in tow isn't a cause for alarm. However, Benny is unpredictable.

"He's not doing me any harm," James says, "but I thought you'd like to know where he is so you won't worry, especially with the weather turning the way it is." He nods at the clouds gathering to the west.

I give him what I hope is a reassuring smile. "Thanks for calling. I did start to worry when he didn't come inside at the first signs of the storm. I didn't realize he'd wandered from the yard, and I was starting to panic when you called."

James raises an eyebrow as if waiting for an explanation, but I don't know what else to say. I rarely understand what goes on inside Benny's head. Neither did my daughter. That's why she abandoned him at the age of three at my doorstep and never came back. The last words Benny heard from his mother were, "I don't know why I got stuck with such a stupid boy. Just call him Ugly. That seems to be the only thing he responds to." After that, she slammed the door, and I cleaned up the puddle of pee that dribbled down Benny's leg and onto the floor. That was the beginning of our adventures together. Most of them have left me haggard through the years as I attempt to reach a little boy who seems so empty inside.

However, this time, serenity replaces the

hollow look that usually resides in Benny's eyes. Although he never expresses emotions through a smile, his face is relaxed. A brewing storm generally sends him hiding under the dirty pile of clothes in his closet, but peace has taken over his whole body. Nothing distracts him from his unexplainable mission.

James holds the gate open for me to go get Benny, but I ignore the gesture. Curiosity leaves me to wonder what my grandson is doing. If this had been the only time Benny had stared at something, then I would just blow off the instance in the urgency of the storm. But it's happened three other times in the past several months under similar circumstances. They all involved him staring at people, and none of them turned out well.

In the first instance, I caught Benny staring at a homeless man at the park. Everyone does that, though usually it's out of the corner of their eyes, not full-on staring the way Benny did it. The second time, Benny couldn't stop staring at a man with Down's Syndrome long enough to pick out a treat at the bakery. I had to pull him away, screaming, without buying him anything.

The last episode was the most embarrassing. My friend Mary graciously took Benny to the library with her daughter so I could have some time alone. But that didn't last. Within twenty minutes she called for me to come to get him.

A girl in a wheelchair fascinated Benny, and he wouldn't stop staring at her. By the time I arrived, many attempts had been made to encourage him to stop. I wasn't any help either. When I tried to move him, he latched onto the girl's wheelchair and started screaming, "Ugly!" I didn't know how to tell the weeping mother that Benny didn't mean anything by it, so I wrestled him off with the help of the janitor and skulked out of the library with him still screaming at the top of his lungs.

When we got home, I lashed out at him in anger. I admit that wasn't my best moment. In my frustration, I yelled at him never to stare at another person again.

He's obeyed that order. Now he's staring at a weed.

The wind picks up. Everything sways in its path, except for my little grandson. Birds scatter overhead with another peal of thunder, and I fight to keep a strand of hair from blowing across my face.

"Shouldn't we get him?" James asks, looking confused. "The storm isn't going to hold off much longer."

I have a choice between interrupting Benny or allowing him to finish what he's started. The former leads to tantrums, and I want to avoid that at all costs.

"This is important to him," I say. "Let's give him just a little longer to see what he does."

James never argues with me, but I can tell he's uncomfortable. While most storms pass without much moisture—more noise than anything—the air is already thick with the smell of rain. A dark mist creeps over the rolling hills, slowly devouring the last of the sun's rays, while lightning replaces the remaining glow with fierce power.

"James, are you there?" A voice crackles over the walkie-talkie on his belt.

He takes it off and answers. "Yes? Come in."

"There are reports of high wind warnings. I wanted to make sure you're headed inside."

"Copy that. I'll be in shortly." James gives me another look as he hooks the walkie-talkie back onto his belt.

"Please, let's give him just a few more minutes," I say, trying to control my begging. Maybe it was my exhaustion from tantrums doing the talking.

"I like to mind my own business, but can you tell me what we're waiting for, Ms. Vivian?" James tilts his cowboy hat lower on his forehead to deflect a raindrop.

I shrug. I'm looking for answers, but since Benny won't tell me what he's doing, I don't know how else to respond. I have to let the scene play out so I can catch a small glimpse as to why he acts this way and hopefully be able to figure out the puzzle of his life on my own.

Minutes pass. Benny still hasn't moved, and I have no idea when or if he'll budge on his own accord. I feel a raindrop. Just one, but I know more are coming. Still I stand there and watch as Benny remains crouched over the weed.

Finally, an eerie fork of lightning is immediately followed by an earsplitting thunderclap. James rubs the back of his neck and sighs. With the storm so close, he seems to have lost faith in my sanity. With that, I know I can't put off getting Benny any longer. At last I decide to interrupt the serenity of this moment.

"I'm ready," I say to James.

He nods as he pulls the gate wider for me to enter. I muster my strength and take a deep breath, mentally preparing myself for a fight. I tiptoe toward Benny. I've learned that I can't move suddenly or raise my voice with impatience. This will be hard to do with the imminent weather controlling the time.

"Hi, sweetheart," I say cautiously, hoping not to trigger a tantrum. I slowly kneel beside Benny. "Are you ready to go?"

It takes a few seconds before Benny moves his eyes to meet mine.

"Song," Benny says and returns his gaze to the weed.

My mind races as I try to figure out what he means. Eight months ago I put Benny into music lessons after he uncovered my mother's piano in the basement. I couldn't get him away from it, so I seized that moment as an opportunity for extra babysitting. Mrs. Jay, his music teacher, takes him every day after school for hour-long lessons. She says that's not even enough time to pour the knowledge of music into Benny at the rate he's absorbing it. He quickly masters any instrument he picks up.

That encrypted word is the only thing Benny says.

"Is that what you want?" I ask. "Do you want to hear a song?"

I'm confused. Before I can explain that not everything is an instrument, Benny rises. I quickly stand with him. A few startled cows moo at us. He's focused on what seems to be a distant thought and isn't bothered by any urgency. He squeezes his eyes shut, then taps his temples with his fingers.

James steps into the field as he prepares to help in any way he can. I look back at him, hoping for a little more patience. He seems to understand the breakthrough, as he stands silent. All we can do is watch and wait. I just wish I'd remembered to bring my sweater before running out the door. The temperature's several degrees cooler than when I first arrived. I shiver with the icy chill of the damp gusts and wonder how long this is going to take to play out.

"Is everything okay?" I ask Benny, hoping not

to push my luck. I rub my arms to warm them up.

Benny begins to nod and sway his head, not in answer to my question, but as if he's lost in the slow, rhythmic beat of another world.

"Song," he repeats between head bobs.

"Tell me about this song."

Benny relaxes his hands and looks at me. He fights to come up with the words. "I made it beauty."

My heart flutters as the picture becomes clearer. Just yesterday, Benny's music teacher approached me after his lesson and gave me a song he'd written. Scrawled across the top in his messy, almost unreadable handwriting were the words, "My Song." He'd scribbled notes across measures in what looked like a non-definable pattern.

"I believe this is for you," Mrs. Jay told me. "Benny tried to explain that this song was for his mom. I know this doesn't look like much, but you need to ask him to play this for you. It's beautiful."

Mrs. Jay smiled at me, her eyes warm. "When Benny first started his lessons, he would throw a tantrum every time I asked him about himself. The only response he would give to me was the word *ugly*. The only way I could settle him down was to play the piano. As I played, I explained to him that every single person has beauty and a purpose, including him. Since then Benny has learned to use music as his voice. Through this song, he's telling his mom about his beauty."

I hadn't had a chance to ask Benny to play his song for me yet. As soon as we got home from his lesson, I was fighting with the daily chores of feeding him, cleaning up after him, trying to bathe him, and getting him ready for bed. With the full evening of exhausting activities, his song never crossed my mind again. Until now.

I fight back the tears as everything begins to make sense. "Benny, will you let Grammy hear its beauty?"

These words are the key that unlocks his world. Benny turns and picks up his violin and bow from the grass and steps back in front of the weed. Most would've overlooked this pathetic, little weed in the scenic majesty of the fields and mountains. Not Benny. He knows the hurt of being disregarded, and he chooses to recognize even a weed's worth in the bigger picture of beauty.

A streak of lightning outlines Benny's figure in a glow. He tilts his head onto the violin's chinrest, and in one smooth motion pulls the bow across the strings. Amid the rolls of distant thunder and howling wind, one long note awakens the pasture. It's strong enough to transform the landscape with its strength, yet subtle enough to soothe the emptiness in my heart.

Many times I'd heard the muffled sound of Benny playing the piano in the basement, but

I'd never stopped to listen. The noise meant he wasn't pulling out the leaves on my houseplants or pouring water into every hole in my house, including the air ducts. It meant relief from running around and putting out fires—thankfully metaphorical ones, at least for now.

The music breathes life into a boy who always seems to be a bother. I stand firm to embrace its fullness and take the time to really listen as the richness of the music weighs the air. In an outpouring of tears, I release my resentment of the years I've spent angry with my daughter for abandoning Benny, the frustration of never knowing how to handle my grandson, and my exhaustion from all the battles. All that disappears.

James rests his hands on my shoulders to join me in the moment. All the distractions of the storm fade as the quivering crescendo ebbs into a beautiful melody that Benny wrote for this weed alone.

A few more scattered drops fall, but none of the notes are dampened. With the weed as its audience and James and me the onlookers, the song proclaims its beauty through a magnificent symphony. The outward appearance of the weed is still brown and withered, but Benny dons it with a brilliance that makes it stand out from the rest of the grass of the field. It's given a brand-new identity seen only through the song.

Now I understand that Benny wasn't staring

at people out of ignorance or wanting to be a bother. He was staring past the labels of this world and redeeming them the only way he knew how. He saw the beauty of the girl in the wheelchair, the homeless man in the park, and the man with Down Syndrome in the bakery and was giving them worth through the beauty of their songs.

With the melody gently tapering, I turn into James's chest and let his shirt absorb my tears. I know he too is submerged in the depth of the music. The wetness of his cheek gives it away.

Then, in one powerful upsurge, the music rises into its apex. Absorbed in the song, Benny dips left and right. His entire body moves to the rhythm that commands the darkness to stave off its threat. The vibrancy of the notes washes everything in their power, and the long last note dissolves into a clap of thunder. Benny lowers the violin, and the heavens open.

Finished with what he's come to do, Benny moves from his spot. He no longer needs coaxing or prodding, and there's no fear of a tantrum. Silently he slips his hand into mine, and we walk out of the field.

Even in the drive of the rain, we don't run or cover our heads. The hurried pace would seem irreverent, as Benny has opened my eyes to the beauty of this world. The fields, the mountains, the raindrops, the people. Nothing is the same. Benny has found his purpose.

CHAPTER 3

Then Sings My Soul

♫

I'd never been inside Ed's house before and wasn't sure what to expect. It was fairly empty. That fit his simplicity. Only one grouping of mismatched furniture finds clustered around a black-and-white television in the farthest corner of the room, while the rest of the green field of shag carpet offered a space large enough to play football. All the sparseness made Ed seem like a squatter in his own home. However, what made everything feel so overwhelmingly intense were the walls. Hundreds of eyes looked down at me as I stood in the middle of his living room: pictures covered the wood paneling from floor to ceiling. Someone had drawn all different kinds of people, and Ed had stuck them up in rows as if it was the latest wallpaper trend. The imbalance of garage sale furniture and museum-quality art would've been tacky—maybe it still was a little—but the perfection of the pictures made up for the huge decorating failure.

In the picture closest to me, a man rode an elephant. The artist captured its gait as it moved in action. I'd tried to draw an elephant once in second grade, but it turned out looking like a gray pig with scoliosis. The only sense of movement mine had was when I threw it into the trashcan. My art teacher said I lacked drawing skills and gave me a U for unsatisfactory. Looking at the animal in front of me, I understood the difference. With its lifelike appearance, that elephant could've walked right out of the picture and into Ed's living room. But even with all those details that competed for my attention, I was drawn to the old man who sat in the scoop of the elephant's neck. His smile struck me the most.

Smiles usually made me uncomfortable. Just the sight of one would send me running in the opposite direction. When I lived with my dad in Alabama, the ongoing joke by the kids at school was that I was a monster. Not the kind with sharp teeth, big claws, and fur that sprouted from everywhere, of course. Although I would've liked it better that way. Then I could've just eaten whoever made fun of me. But that wasn't the case. I was a monster because my face had taken the brunt of my dad's abuse.

What fascinated me about the man's smile

in the picture was that it didn't make fun of me. Instead, I bloomed under his gaze. The only time I'd ever felt that sensation was when my mama was alive. Her reassuring smile always gave me comfort. The man's gaze pulled out that long-forgotten feeling of my mama's love buried behind layers of fear and shame. I stood grounded in its power, relishing the nurturing glow. His eyes saw past my brokenness and didn't judge me. With one look, he connected with my pain, yet his smile implied he knew happiness.

The creak of the kitchen door startled me, and I spun to face Ed.

He stuck his head out around the door. "Johnny, would you l-like some cookies with your l-lemonade?" Ed asked.

The right side of his face sagged, causing his wrinkles to droop into a pile beside his lips. The added weight dragged his speech just enough for me to have to listen more closely. It didn't help, either, that it looked like he'd stolen his teeth from a whale.

"Sure," I said. "Do you need any help?"

Ed thoughtfully shook his head. "I don't h-have guests often. We'll vi-sit in a minute."

He closed the kitchen door behind him, leaving me alone once again to marvel at the unusual, remarkable sight around me. I thought I knew Ed, at least at the I'll-share-my fries-with-you level. However, the pictures showed a side of him I'd never seen before. I must've spent more time talking about my stolen gym shorts and how I avoided swirlies at school than asking him meaningful questions. I was new to the whole friend thing. As it was, it'd taken me seven of the ten months I'd lived in Mississippi to get the courage to approach Ed.

It was hard for me to meet new people. Almost impossible. But even though Ed was old, I was drawn to him. While Ed repulsed others by his behaviors, I found him safe, and he became my only friend. Frank Skylanders didn't count. Although we sat at the same lunch table, we never talked to each other.

Ed and I weren't like that. All we did was talk. At least that was all I ever did. We met at the diner every week, and I dumped useless information onto him as if it'd been bottled up for centuries, waiting to be poured out onto anyone who'd listen. No one else knew that my favorite band was the Rolling Stones or that I dreamed of playing major league baseball one day or that I had a crush on Lizzie Stephens. All the while, Ed would sit quietly across from me at the diner, sipping his milkshake and making me feel as though I could do anything I dreamed.

Ed had arrived in Buford just a few months before I came. That was the only important thing I knew about him, but no one knew where he'd been before that. That unknown fact labeled him suspicious by the town's people. Ms. Lettie, my aunt's beautician, said he'd escaped from a mental institution—oddly enough, with her raccoon eyes and lipstick smeared up to her nose, it looked as if she belonged in one. The truth rarely came out of her mouth, so to me, that proved Ed had more sanity than she did. Minus the lies, that was about the extent of what I knew about Ed. He kept to himself and spent his days walking up Pine Street, down Church, and through the park. I spent a lot of time watching him from Uncle Clancy's hardware store, where I helped sweep to get ice cream money.

The pictures on the wall were the only real clues to the mystery of Ed. In one, a girl danced in a ceremonial costume. With one hand raised above her head, she flared her dress with the other. In another, a lady with dark skin balanced a water jug on her head. A baby was peacefully swaddled against her back, while goats and chickens cleared a path for her to walk. Every person had the same knowing look and encouraging smile as the man who rode the elephant. What interested me the most was that the people came from every background, age, and culture. The hint of adventure was strange, because with his beat-up, good-for-nothing shoes, Ed didn't look like he'd traveled much past the Chickasaw county line.

Ed waddled back into the room, carrying a tray with a pitcher of lemonade, two glasses, and two plates piled with cookies. He walked hunched, as if someone had shoved him over and he'd gotten stuck that way. The sway of his walk coupled with his trembling hands caused the ice to clink. I took one last glance at the pictures and followed him over to the couch.

"You've dis-covered my treasures," Ed said. "I thought you'd enjoy them. That's why I invited you to my h-house today. I thought it was time to sh-show off my most precious posses-sions to you. I'm glad you accepted my invitation."

I felt honored that he felt close enough to share with me as I did with him. I wasn't sure about that since he let me do the talking most of the time.

"I've never seen anything quite like them. They all look real and like they have something they want to tell me. The man on the elephant made me feel as though I could carry on a conversation with him."

Ed nodded. "Go ah-head and give it a try. I do it all the time. All my friends are such great com-pany."

"Uh, no, that's ok. Thanks."

I tried to ignore the sudden fear that crept up in my belly as I saw into my future as a lonely old man, talking to a bunch of pictures on the wall and calling them my friends. I didn't want to be like Ed, whose humming and muttering drove people to the other side of the street to avoid contact with him.

"Suit yours-self," he said.

Ed set everything on the coffee table. I sat on the plastic-covered couch, while he sat in a folding chair next to me. I picked up the plate of cookies in front of me, grabbed one, and took a bite. With his curled fingers, Ed fumbled for the jug and poured us both a glass of lemonade. Some missed and dribbled down the sides. After the tedious task, Ed handed me a glass.

"This sh-should cool us down a bit," he said.

"Thank you." I shoved the rest of the cookie into my mouth and took the lemonade.

Ed unfolded a napkin across his lap and settled into his routine of counting the chocolate chips in his cookie. He needed at least seven before he would eat it. It was because of that habit that I highly recommended for him to drink milkshakes at the diner. Our conversations became much easier after he switched.

I interrupted when he got to five. "Who are all these people?"

Ed set the cookie back on the plate and brushed off his hands. "The-se are the people I've m-met during my travels."

I stalled taking a sip of lemonade and left the glass tilted in front of my lips. "You've met all these people?"

Ed seemed unfazed by my shock as he smoothed the napkin in his lap.

I'd only seen him by himself but tried to imagine what it would be like for Ed to meet all these people. Every person on the wall looked confident, as if they had other important jobs to do rather than meeting a social misfit. I, on the other hand, was just like Ed. My first encounter with him consisted of me gawking at my feet while he stared at the top of my head for several minutes. I was desperate to make a friend, so I endured the awkwardness. However, I had a hard time believing that any of the people on the walls would've gone through the same effort. Out of curiosity, I dug deeper.

I sipped my drink. "I didn't know you liked to travel."

"Trav-eling's part of my job."

"Oh." I'd never seen Ed do anything but walk around town. "Well, you've certainly been to a lot of places."

"I h-have," Ed said, picking up the cookie with five chips.

He started over with his count. This time I focused on the drawing above his head while I waited for him to finish. A boy sat cross-legged in a crowded market. He couldn't have been much older than me and seemed about as mischievous. The details of the market created a busy scene with a noise I could almost hear. But another faint sound vibrating beneath the background caught my attention. I leaned closer to the picture to listen.

After counting eleven chips, Ed took a bite. "Choc-olate chip is my favorite kind of cookie. You can't sk-skimp on the chips."

I pulled myself from the picture of the boy to encounter Ed noisily gulping the lemonade as he washed down the one bite of cookie. He put the glass back in its exact ring of condensation on the table. I'd gotten used to all his quirks but wondered how he fit in other cultures.

"What's it like to visit other places?" I asked. "I mean, far off ones. I've often dreamed about going to the places I've read about. Reading is about the only time I get to escape reality. I want to visit another country, the moon, or even go under the sea. But the farthest I've been is to Buford, and I can't say it's been all that great. Just the smell from Dugan's processing plant alone is enough to make me want to run away and never come back."

Ed's laugh sounded like a wheezing walrus. "You're r-right," he said, catching his breath. "It does smell bad here. I th-thought the same thing when I arrived. When you l-ive here, you get used to it, but even on hot days, nobody w-wants to open their windows on the west side. All places have their pros and cons, even far off ones, I suppose. However, no matter where I go, it's the people who m-make the place special."

Maybe that was why I struggled in my new

home. I didn't think people were all that great, let alone made the place special. People were a lot easier to love in books because they never actually said anything back. Maybe that was why I liked the drawings so much. They were quiet, didn't judge, and gave me a taste of adventure all at the same time.

I wondered how Ed was able to meet all the beautiful people on the walls. He was ugly. I was ugly. We'd never really talked about how different we were from everyone else, but my curiosity overrode the sensitive topic.

"So"—I let out a breath—"when you're in other places, do people still make fun of you? I've just never been good at meeting people. It's hard because I'm not like everyone else. I've learned that not many people understand people like . . . well, people like us, if you know what I mean." I ran the last few words together, trying to get them out without offense.

A murmur of studio laughter rose from the television in front of us. I'd ignored it until then but was thankful for the relief the lightheartedness gave.

"I underst-stand," Ed said over the petering applause.

I relaxed, picked up another cookie, and stuffed the whole thing in my mouth. I wiped the crumbs from my lips with my sleeve.

Ed laid his hands across his chest, and the

gnarled mass rose and fell with his breath. "People still judge me no matter where I am. That truth is always the same, but I don't focus on th-that. Instead, I search for those who want to be known. Those are the peop-le I meet on my journeys. That's why we met, isn't it, John-ny? You wanted to be known?"

I'd never thought of it that way before, but Ed was right. I craved the attention he gave me. Aunt Mae and Uncle Clancy didn't really know me; I was just the abused nephew who needed help. With their overdoting, make-everything-better sort of way, they loved me, and I appreciated it. However, Ed was different. I could be myself around him and not be either a monster or a victim. He listened to know me for who I was on the inside.

I picked at the edge of the paper plate. "I thought my life would be different once I moved to Buford, but people still make fun of me. Even adults. Ms. Lettie told everyone I had some kind of infectious disease they'd catch if they hung around me for too long. That's why all the old ladies walked around town with handkerchiefs covering their noses for weeks. If only they knew how stupid they looked. When Aunt Mae overheard some of them talking about it at bingo night at church, she threw a tantrum and set them all straight. I would've liked to have seen her throw Mrs. Hassel's card and chips on the floor."

I went to laugh but couldn't. It ended up as a heaving sigh as I leaned back, laid my head against the couch, and stared at the glitter in the popcorn ceiling. I was tense but couldn't even relax in the heat of the house. The wave of air from the fan didn't quite reach me. Sweat stuck me into place on the plastic lining of the couch, highlighting my discomfort.

"I'm s-sorry for how much that hurts," Ed said. "Ms. L-lettie can create some wild stories with her imagination. I don't think she understands how bad-ly they can hurt."

"If they sound so ridiculous, why do people believe them?"

"We all carry h-hurt in some form or another, and people will be-lieve anything to take the attention off their own pain. Ms. Lettie's de-fense mechanism is telling stories about others. It makes her f-eel better about herself. However, if you knew the pain she's gone th-through, you may see her dif-ferently. I know it's hard to understand, but Ms. Lettie does have beauty."Finding her beauty would've been like searching for a one-karat diamond in a mud pit the size of Florida.

On the wall I noticed a picture of a lady who wore a crown and stood under an ornate chandelier in a ballroom. I sat up. Now, she had beauty. I scrutinized her smile against the others. To me, it was the sweetest; then again, I found her the most attractive. It felt like she spoke to me with words only my heart could understand. I heard them as they quickened my pulse but couldn't interpret them. Though I first thought it was foolishness when Ed said that he talked to the pictures, I had to admit I wouldn't mind it so much to carry on a conversation with her.

"Is she royalty?" I pointed to the lady.

Pausing in reaching for his glass, Ed looked up and turned. "Ah, you've f-found Adina. She *is* royalty and quite fas-cinating."

"How did you meet someone like her?"

I realized how rude that sounded. My cheeks grew hot, and I couldn't meet Ed's eyes. I stared at the wave of shag carpet beneath my feet.

"I don't mean nothing bad by that," I said, fumbling. I looked back at Ed, who just smiled. "She just seems so—"

"I know." Ed nodded. "I bel-ieve the word you're looking for is perfect. But nobody's perfect. We all try to ap-pear that way on the outside. Sadly, some think they've suc-ceeded in fooling people, but if they'd only realize how much that pr-ide highlights their flaws. But those who understand their imperfections are the ones who dis-cover true beauty."

"What do you mean?" I set my plate of cookies and glass of lemonade on the coffee table to give him my full attention.

"Well, may-be it would help you to under-stand by knowing that Adina is a lot like y-you."

I'd only dreamed of looking that good. My secret wish was to look like David Cassidy. Even Ed didn't know that about me.

"It doesn't look like we're anything alike," I said, glancing back at her.

"It's because you d-don't know her story."

"Then what is it?"

Ed closed his eyes and creased his forehead. His entire body relaxed as he began to hum a tune I'd never heard before. His hands rose as if he conducted a melody, and he lost himself in another world. Anyone looking through the window would've thought he'd lost his mind. However, no matter how crazy it looked, being in his house, in his world, I felt more connected to him than I'd ever been before. I wanted to go with him to where the melody began. It was a place of peace that tugged me to join. A tear escaped his squinted eyes.

I wasn't new to emotions that made me cry; fear and loneliness were just some of them. However, as I watched Ed, an unfamiliar feeling overcame me. I wanted to cry because I was experiencing something wonderful, something I couldn't explain or put words to. Just as my emotions were heightened, he began.

"I'll do my b-best to tell Adina's story properly." Ed opened his moist eyes. "I was there the first time she dis-covered water bubbling over rocks in a creek and the cool sensation of moss sliding be-tween the toes. She abandoned herself to childlike gid-diness as she explored the world she'd never known."

Ed smiled fondly. "But I'm getting ahead of my-self. I met Adina in a small village in France a l-long, long time ago. She was the daughter of a wealthy merchant. That may seem like a good l-life—and it should've been—but her father kept her locked inside the h-house."

I knew how that felt. My own dad had used a chair to wedge me inside my bedroom closet. He'd beat me if I made any sound while different girls came over. It was almost like if I weren't seen or heard, then I poofed into nonexistence. Shame met me in the darkness, and I wondered if Adina shared that same empty feeling that nagged my memories. My heart ached for her.

"I don't understand," I said. "Why did he do that? I know I acted out, but she doesn't look like she would deserve something that bad."

Sorrow crossed Ed's face, and he shook his head. "Oh, John-ny, no one deserves to be beaten or forgotten. It doesn't mat-ter how someone looks or what they've done. Being beaten may have been normal f-for you, but that doesn't mean you deserved it. This world hurts people with its lies, and that's what happened to A-dina too."

Ed scratched his ear and then refolded his hands on his chest. "Adina was born with a sp-ine so curved that she could barely walk, and her father was ashamed of that. He had hopes for his daughter to mar-ry well and to live a good life. Those hopes ended the day she was b-born. His embarrassment made him believe that no m-man would want her, and because of that, he told Adina that she could never leave the house. St-ories told by the servants brought about tales that had people stumbling over themselves to catch an-y sight of the deformed girl who lived behind the walls. Her life became a cir-cus sideshow."

"Then how did you meet her?" I asked.

"One day I was out walk-ing when a fierce storm came on suddenly. I was far from where I lived and need-ed shelter. I knocked on the gates that lined the street, but everyone t-turned me away. No one wanted to help someone like me. However, Adina saw my plight from her bed-room window and sent word to her servant that she was to let me inside and ca-re for me.

"When I knock-ed on her father's gate, the servant res-cued me. I was led inside, where she dried me off, cook-ed me a meal, and offered me a place to stay for the night. When I thanked her for the kind-ness, she told me that her master was the one who took p-ity on me. However, when I asked to speak to her master, Adina wouldn't c-come to meet me. She was too ashamed, because she believed she was unworthy to m-meet anyone."

I always knew the power that words held over me, but it was unfathomable how they could destroy even the most beautiful human being.

"It wasn't un-til I ventured out of my room later that night that I was able to catch a gl-impse of her. Even in the darkness of the hallway, Adina's beauty str-uck me. She hid in the shadows, watching me with gr-eat curiosity. For the first time, she was seeing someone m-much like herself. My looks became the bridge to our meeting.

"I spent se-veral more weeks at her house. During our times together, I helped her to see her real beauty. It wasn't l-ong after I left that Adina was on one of her new ad-ventures when she caught the eye of the prince who hap-pened to be passing through her village. They married, and he la-ter took the throne. That's why a merchant girl wears that cr-crown. Queen Adina's compassion made her the most beloved qu-een France had ever seen."

I squinted at Adina, searching for any flaw. "She doesn't look like she has a disability to me."

"Of c-course not," Ed said. "I never saw her as having a dis-ability."

"Then the picture doesn't show who she is."

"On the con-trary, that picture shows you exactly who sh-e is. All it took was bringing her beauty to l-ife."

"Then who drew it?"

"I d-id."

I tried not to glance at Ed's fingers and ended

up staring intensely at his chin. "How did . . ." I squirmed. "Sorry."

A smile tugged the droop of Ed's lips. "I listen for the beauty that's in the stories of those a-round me. Most artists train their eye on the out-side and draw with perfection the details of what they see. S-such excellence produces great artwork, but that's not what I do. I don't w-want to recreate imperfection. Instead, I train my ears on the inside and l-isten to the song of each soul, and that beauty becomes my masterpiece. It doesn't take strong hands to do that. It takes a str-ong heart."

Ed leaned forward, and instinctively, I leaned forward with him.

"I even k-now your song, John-ny," he said.

"I have a song?" It seemed like an exhilarating promise, but doubt crept into my voice. "Uh, how come I've never heard it?"

"The w-world drowns it out. But I hear it even now. I love be-ing caught up in its greatness."

Ed's gaze turned distant, and he gently swayed to a melody I yearned to hear. I closed my eyes and listened harder than I ever had. The oscillating fan on the stool banged against the wall as it remained stuck in its position. A car revved outside. The gallop of the Lone Ranger's horse syncopated the seconds. But no song.

Disappointed, I opened my eyes. "Will I ever be able to hear it?"

Ed looked back at me. "That's why I invited you here. I wanted to give you the gift of your song. It'll a-dd the beauty to your story that you've been search-ing for."

"But there's nothing beautiful about my story."

"You're right, th-ere's not. I'm sorry about your dad's abuse, and I can't take that away. But the song takes your story with a-ll its brokenness and transforms it into some-thing new."

"I don't understand. How does it work?"

"I l-isten to your song and draw who you are through its brill-iance. When you see your true self, th-en you and the world around you will be forever changed. W-would you like that?"

"Is that what you did for all these other people?" I asked. "You allowed them to see themselves through their song?"

"It is."

I hadn't felt beautiful for a long time. I wanted so badly to catch a glimpse of what that would look like but oddly feared it too. I didn't just want a picture of what I'd look like with beauty; I wanted to be beautiful. I glanced at those who'd gone before me. When I looked again at Adina, I felt a surge of encouragement.

"If you draw me, will you put my picture next to Adina's?" I asked.

"I'll def-initely do that for you."

"Ok. Then I want it."

Ed rubbed his hands together. "That's wonderful. You won't regret it. I have to get a few things before w-e begin."

Ed stood and went to a storage closet and brought out an easel and a briefcase.

"Give me a m-moment," he said. "I have to get ready."

Ed set his briefcase beside the tray of cookies and lemonade. He spread the contents onto the coffee table and went through his routine of rearranging their order before being satisfied. He rolled up his sleeves, sat in his chair, and pulled the easel toward himself. He then picked up the pencil closest to him. Even with all his deformities that would've kept most from drawing at all, at that moment, his confidence gave him the look of a natural artist.

"I'm read-y," Ed said. "Now tell me your story."

Without me even acknowledging my story, it haunted, mocked, and defined me. But I wasn't sure if I knew how to—or even wanted to—give it words.

"Where do I start?" I asked. "The day I began my transformation into a monster?"

Ed nodded. "That's a g-good place as any to st-start." He hunched behind the easel, ready to start.

"Ok. I'll do my best."

I took a deep breath to clear my mind, and

as soon as I closed my eyes, the echoes of my past whispered their frightening memories. *Come here, Johnny.* My dad's voice rang in my thoughts, and I clasped my ears to block it out. My dad's form flickered on the back of my eyelids like a bad movie. He teetered at the front door with a beer can in one hand and a cigarette in the other.

"It was the day of my mama's funeral," I slowly began. "After the service, my dad left me alone. I'm not sure how long he was gone, but I sat long enough on the living room floor for it to get dark outside. When he finally came back, the headlights from his old truck shone through the window when he missed the driveway and parked across the yard. He threw open the door, stumbled inside, and demanded me to come."

Even after four years, those details were still suspended in my mind like they were stuck in a glob of Jell-O. I missed my mom all over again. If she'd never died, none of this would've ever happened. I knew it. My dad left after the funeral service to deal with his demons and came home a different person. That vacant spot in my heart that nothing else could fill started to ache all over again.

Out of the stabbing pain, a quiet hum broke through the turmoil of my thoughts. Its sole job felt like it was to prepare my heart for the onslaught of something more. I embraced its fullness and held onto it like a lifeline. The comfort it gave kept me going.

I placed my hands on each side of me to brace for further pain. Ed's humming overpowered everything else.

"I knew by the sound of my dad's voice he wasn't looking for a hug, so I jumped up and ran. The only head start I had from his anger was when he collapsed against the wall and took a few minutes to gather himself. I used that time to crawl under the kitchen sink to hide. I pressed my knees to my chest, buried my head between my legs, and prayed the only prayer I knew — 'now I lay me down to sleep.' My mama had taught me to say that prayer before bedtime each night. I just figured God would sort out the words according to the situation."

While I'd been, talking the fullness of a song had slipped into my story. I hadn't noticed it until I stopped to catch my breath. A chorus of notes had joined the hum, creating a symphony that engulfed the room. The breathtaking music took the painful memories and sifted through them with its tune as if plucking them to toss them out.

Overwhelmed by its power, I sobbed. The song continued, filling in the gaps between my gasps. I sat in its strength until I was able to gather myself and begin again.

"Even though I tried to keep quiet, my daddy already knew where I hid. That was my usual hiding spot when I played hide-and-seek with Mama—sometimes I hid behind the dining room curtain, but I couldn't get to it in time. My mama had always walked past me during games and acted as though she didn't see me. Now she was gone, and my daddy didn't play that way. I heard his cowboy boots stop right outside my hiding space, and before the door barely opened, he grabbed my arm and yanked me out."

Boy! What did you do? My dad's words, a deep, guttural growl, throbbed inside my head. I cowered in the chair as if bracing for the impact I knew was coming. The emotion of being pulled back through the pain broke the dam with my tears. The song released its force in a melodic roar as it saturated my words, cleansing the pain. It rushed over me before settling into a hush that quieted my uncontrollable breaths. I rested in its comfort. When I began again, a tremor commanded my voice.

"My daddy blamed me for my mama's death. Even at six years old, I couldn't convince him otherwise. As I dangled from his grip, I somehow knew my life wouldn't be the same. I was right. It wasn't. He crushed the beer can with one hand and slapped it across my head. That blow knocked me to the ground."

I rubbed my finger over the divot of my first scar above my right eyebrow. Many others surrounded it.

"Now I'm a monster," I said.

The hurt and pain eased into tears that rolled down my cheeks. The saltiness ran into my mouth, and I didn't bother to spit it out. I sniffed and peeked.

I could see Ed from the side while he drew. He was absorbed in the depth of his work while the room reeled peacefully around me. I felt each note deep within my bones. Several times, he twisted and contorted. I felt the stinging jolts of his movements like we were connected. Each time it was over, he would continue. The sight of Ed at work brought me peace. The song swallowed all other sounds, and the vibration was powerful enough to soothe the hurt.

Although I'd lived for so long with the nightmare of all those memories, I felt relieved to have said them out loud. In an emotional outpouring of my soul, I conquered them. But one fact still remained.

"I don't want to be different anymore." I sank into the stiff cushions of the couch. "I want to feel what it's like to be normal."

Ed's eyes momentarily rose above the canvas as if wordlessly acknowledging what I'd said. He then went back to work. His head bobbed up and down as he scribbled. He grabbed his cheek and grimaced. At the same time, I felt my own shot of pain in my cheek. This happened several times. His arms shook as the easel rocked back and forth. Although the motion was violent, the music eased into a stillness that emanated from the canvas. The tap and scrape of his work almost covered it.

"I guess that's all I have to say." I rubbed the wetness off my nose and mouth with my sleeve.

While I waited for Ed to finish, I stared out the window. It was as if it was a different life. The world remained unchanged outside the window. A hummingbird tapped on the feeder, and a magnolia tree offered shade to the west side of the house. The world really did have beauty. I'd never really recognized it before. I let Ed do his thing as I stared through the blinds.

After a while, Ed finally spoke while making exaggerated marks on the page. "Trage-dy and brokenness are part of everyone's st-story. Some wear it in the form of shame or bitter-ness. Others mask it with pride or detachment. No one knows what to do with it, so it becomes the cords that str-angle the beauty inside us. Life dims it until we've for-gotten what it looks like. So the soul has to be reminded of its w-worth."

With that, Ed relaxed. His motionless form commanded the song to dissipate, but everything was still affected by it.

"W-would you like to see what I've drawn?" he asked.

"Yes," I whispered as suspense nearly took my breath away.

Ed turned the work of art toward me. In the

picture, I stood on a pitching mound, holding a ball in one hand and cupping it with a glove with the other. My face was perfect. No scars remained. My image looked back with a huge smile as if it knew a secret it longed to tell me.

"Wow," I said, not able to stop staring. "I look so different without my scars."

"That's w-ho you really are."

"I wish I really did look like that. Then I might have a chance with Lizzy Stephens."

"I h-have a feeling Lizzy will notice you soon e-nough."

I narrowed my eyes. "Say, why did you draw me playing baseball? I don't play anymore. I mean, I dream of playing again, but not even the neighborhood kids want me on their team. Not like this."

Ed nodded knowingly. "All t-hat'll change soon enough."

He stood to clean up the mess. The afternoon light filtering through the blinds bathed him in light. When I saw him in that glow, I gasped. His face looked like mine. He had the nose that set crooked from too many breaks. His right eyelid hung limp. And his mouth was pulled down into a permanent scowl.

"Why do you look like me?" I asked.

"Act-ually, you're now the reflection of who I am. G-go and see for yourself."

"What?"

I slapped my hands over my face and scrubbed my cheeks. It was clean from pockmarks and bumps. I jumped up, ran to the mirror over the sideboard, and rubbed over the smoothness. I stared in disbelief.

"What happened?" I asked.

"I t-took everything away that hindered you from seeing the beau-ty of who you are. You still have the same st-story, but now I own your ugliness."

"Why do you own my ugliness?"

I lowered my hands as I realized I no longer looked like a monster. The newfound freedom from my old identity left me weak with delight. No one had ever done anything for me like that before.

"I didn't w-want you to have to be burdened with it anymore, and I'm the on-ly one who can handle it."

"But why me?"

"You l-looked past my outward appearance to see that I had more to of-fer. No one else was brave enough to do that."

I'd spent that first year of my abuse crying into my pillow and wishing for a different life. My favorite children's book my mama used to read to me was about the metamorphosis of a butterfly. Unfortunately, that process was all backward for me. I'd gotten uglier and uglier, and there was nothing I could do to stop it. My prayers had run dry long before my tears had stopped. I couldn't do anything to stop that change. It was hard to believe that in just one afternoon all my ugliness was gone. Joy fought through my astonishment and shook my knees with delight. I'd been changed just like that butterfly!

"I don't know what to say," I said. "This is more than what I could've ever hoped for. Thank you for such a wonderful gift."

Ed paused from folding up the easel. "Oh, John-ny, I'm more than happy to do that for you, but heal-ing your scars wasn't my gift to you. That's just an ex-tra benefit of allowing your song to intertwine with mine."

"I don't understand. If that wasn't the gift, then what is it?"

Ed smiled. "I'll demon-strate it for you."

He set down the easel, and in his limp-step fashion, he walked to the wall and placed his hand on a picture of a man who was resting his head on a pitchfork. He motioned for me to come to his side. When I did, he took my hand and placed it on the frame under his.

"Now list-en with your heart," he said, leaning in with expectancy.

I closed my eyes, and a rich orchestra of brass, winds, and strings encircled me. The staccato notes made my heart dance. The music was better than discovering a hidden treasure from deep inside a cereal box. This wasn't cheap like a decoder ring or spyglasses. This had value I'd never known, and I wanted to hang onto it as long as possible.

"This is Gio-vanni's song." Ed's voice heightened with excitement as he squeezed my shoulder with his other hand. "Isn't it a-mazing?"

It was. I could barely pull myself away. "I can hear it! His song is nothing like mine."

"You're r-ight. No two songs are a-like."

"Why can I hear his song?"

Ed's eyebrows rose. "Oh, it's n-not just his song you can hear. Now you can hear the songs of all th-ose around you. The world is a beautiful symphony, waiting to be h-heard. That gift transforms you more than having any change in your outward appearance. No long-er will you see people through the masks they wear, but you'll hear their beauty through their souls. The r-eal gift is compassion and love. Amazing things will happen when y-ou look at someone in that way. Lives will change, and Bu-ford needs that."

I saw compassion in Ed. He loved people despite how badly they treated him. I looked back at all the pictures. Although I'd never met any of those people, I felt connected to every one of them like they were somehow family.

"So, all these people really are like me."

"Yes, they all suf-fered in some kind of way, whether it was physical, emotional, or mental. They h-had nowhere else to turn but to me. Since

I took their burdens and they were no longer w-weighed down by them, they learned to love those around them. They even l-learned to love the ones that had hurt th-em the most."

I wasn't sure how I would love the ones that had hurt me the most. "I hope you gave this gift to the right person."

Ed patted my back. "I d-did. This town doesn't need me anymore. Since they now have you, I'll be leaving s-soon."

"Wait a minute, you're leaving? You can't do that! I can't do this by myself. You're my only friend."

"That w-on't be true for long. You're stronger than you realize. I c-ame here for you to discover true beauty, and my j-job is finished. Others need me, just like you did. How-ever, you won't be lonely anymore. People will be drawn to you. Not to mention, you're part of me. When I m-move on to the next place, you'll be part of my collection, and I'll put you up right next to Adina."

I hugged Ed and tried not to cry. He put his arm around my shoulder and drew me close.

"Your first steps outside will be the most incredible moments you'll ever have. And I want to be there for them."

Keeping his arm around my shoulder, Ed walked me to the door and opened it. "Go a-head," he urged.

I stood on the front porch. Although Ed had

said those first steps outside would be wonderful, I still wasn't prepared for what I heard. It was like I walked into a world where a musical hum held up the undercurrents of everything around me. It took my anger and remorse and set them free.

I turned my ear down the street to where Ms. Lettie walked her dog. She waved at me and pasted on a smile. Although that fakeness would've normally set me on edge, something different happened. In the warmth of the afternoon sun, a beautiful song penetrated the air, and understanding of her hurt filled the place where I once held bitterness. The song gave me a glimpse past her defenses and transformed how I saw her. Underneath it all, Ms. Lettie begged for people to see her differently, too, just like I had. Tears of joy ran down my cheeks as I saw her true beauty for the first time.

I waved back and genuinely smiled. I finally understood the depth of what Ed did for this town and me. I had a gift to give the people, one I had to receive first in order to understand.

CHAPTER 4

Through the Eyes of Hero George

♫

I added one last scribble to the end of Hero George's cape and added the caption, "And remember, Johnny, you have a purpose. All you have to do is find it." Hero George's hands were planted stoically on his hips as he gave that final monologue. I made his right arm a little longer to match his left and then shoved the colored pencil back into the pouch and zipped it up.

Mama gently knocked on the door and let herself into my room. "Babem, are you still doing okay?"

I tucked my journal under my pillow and nodded.

Mama came to my side. "I called Dr. Juni. She said you're going to be just fine. The glue is nontoxic. You do understand that it's normal for you to lose your teeth, right? You don't have to try to put them back in. Others grow in to take their place."

I shrugged. I didn't think she understood the horror of what I'd glimpsed in the black-and-white photograph of Babem Ulgive Oxenbow II, one of my unfortunate namesakes. I'd seen his picture when Mama and I were looking through an old photo album that morning. Saying the toothless old man with one big unibrow was ugly was an understatement.

With that horrific image emblazoned on my mind, I was certain my fate had begun when I bit into an apple later that day and my front tooth fell out. After running to my room, I sobbed uncontrollably as I tried for hours to glue the tooth back into its socket. Mama would never have known of the incident if she hadn't brought my freshly folded laundry into my room and I hadn't vomited—right onto her feet—the whole bottle of glue I'd swallowed while attempting to save my image.

"Is there something else on your mind?" she asked. "You haven't seemed to be yourself all day."

There was. Mama was blessed with listening ears. She had to have them to interpret what I tried to say. Those ears granted her patience and compassion when my tongue wouldn't cooperate. During those times it would, at best, translate my thoughts into a mess that sounded like a broken helicopter rotor.

"Th-th-this m-morning y-yoo-u t-told m-m-me I h-had a pur-purpo-se," I uttered after many pauses, breaths, and contorted faces. "I d-don't kn-know w-w-what it i-is."

Before the incident with the photo album, I'd sat for hours contemplating what my purpose was supposed to be. Billy Honor's dad was a firefighter. That was pretty cool. He came to my class one day and demonstrated how to use all the equipment. Everyone clapped and had fun. My dad was a traveling salesman. Thank goodness he didn't come to class. But neither one of those things seemed to fit me.

"Oh, Babem," Mama said, sighing. "You don't have to find out what your purpose is today. I just want you to understand how special you are. You're not like Babem Ulgive Oxenbow the first or second."

That was a relief.

Mama placed a hand on my head and smiled. "You're you and not a mistake. All the pieces of your life will come together and will make sense one day. You'll see. You just keep living each day as the best Babem Ulgive Oxenbow III there is. Be proud of who you are. With a name like that you can't help but be great." After the last line, she kissed my forehead, turned out the light, and left me to wonder why my dad, Daniel Porter Oxenbow, would reinstate such an atrocious name.

In the light of the moon, I pulled my journal back out from underneath my pillow and opened it. I grabbed a pencil off the nightstand and scrawled the words "Wanting a Purpose" across the top of the *Hero George* cartoon frames and added the date: March 20, 1971.

September 24–25, 1971: The Punch

"I-I-I r-r-a-a-a-n fa-fast todaa-aay," I said proudly.

"That doesn't surprise me," Mama said as she brought me a glass of milk and set it next to the plate of meatloaf. "You have legs like your father."

Great. Legs like a stork.

"He was the fastest kid in high school," she went on to explain. "He was even the state champion in the mile both his junior and senior years. There wasn't anyone around who could catch him."

Hearing that made me feel a little better, although I couldn't picture my dad as a runner.

Mama sat next to me and began to eat her supper. "What made you run so fast?"

Uh-oh. That was an innocent question, but it was then I realized I'd made a mistake to reference my running ability. The true story was that I punched Bobby, my classmate, and then outran him. I hid inside the neighbor's doghouse until Bobby gave up looking for me.

"M-m-my d-d-a-y at sc-sc-h-ool w-w-was h-h-ha-hard." I stuffed a big forkful of mashed potatoes in my mouth to keep from having to explain.

"Oh, I see," Mama said, not letting it go. "I'm not sure how a rough day in second grade can make you run so fast. Is there anything more?"

She did the pointed stare-over-the-glass-without-taking-a-sip look until I explained the events that led up to me running fast.

School was always rough, but particularly on that day. First off, we had a substitute teacher who insisted on calling out everyone by his or her full name. Most teachers had sweet mercy. Not Ms. Lulander.

"Bay-bem. Bah-bem. Ul-give. Yulegive. Oxenbow." Ms. Lulander raised the roll book to within inches of her nose and readjusted her glasses, as if that would somehow miraculously help produce the right pronunciation.

She was determined to get it right. She gave a long pause, and the class went silent, as if waiting for the delivery of the punch line. They didn't have to wait long.

"Now, Mr. Oxenbow, is your first name pronounced baa, baa, Babem like a sheep, or bay-bay Baybem like a baby?"

Really? She had to ask that?

I didn't have to answer. The whole class

started making sheep noises as I shrank down in my seat. I knew this would be used against me. Sure enough, it was.

"Baa-Baa-Babem is a bay-bay-baby," Bobby whispered.

I wanted to bah-bah-bop him.

After several more laughs, Ms. Lulander settled the class down and managed to make it through the rest of the names on the list with ease. But then, names like Hank Porter and Sally White weren't really that hard to pronounce.

"All right, everyone. Now that roll call is over, it's time for our science review. I want everyone quiet and all eyes on me. I'm going to go through the roll book and ask each one of you a question. Answer it correctly and you'll get a free cookie at lunch today. Doesn't that sound lovely?"

If being thrown into a cage of lions with meat around my neck was lovely, then yes. Mrs. Yammick, our real teacher, always played games to help us study. That meant I didn't have to say anything. Ms. Lulander didn't get the memo that if a teacher needed to know something, they'd talk to me privately. No one ever made me talk out loud. One by one the students were called, and many cookies were given out. Then it was my turn.

"Babem," Ms. Lulander said with obvious pride after saying my name properly. "What object in the sky reflects the sun's light?"

People snickered before I could answer.

That was easy. It was the moon. I could say it in my head, but after a few clicks of the tongue, it came out, "mo-mo-er, er-ooonnnn."

Silence. Then it came.

"Baa-baa-Babem the bay-bay baby is a mo-mo-moron," shouted Bobby from the back row.

He sounded more like a moron than I did, but nobody else saw it that way. The whole class erupted in laughter, and Ms. Lulander couldn't settle them back down before recess. The rest of the day was lost in whispered taunts of "baa-baa-Babem the bay-bay baby is a mo-mo-moron" with Bobby leading the others. I had yet to develop a tolerance for teasing.

I wanted Bobby to taste embarrassment, so after we got off the school bus, I walked to where he congregated with his friends and laid a right hook across his jaw. It was a technique I'd never tried, and I was surprised it actually worked. Bobby fell back on impact and landed in a holly bush. But the one thing I didn't expect was how quickly Bobby could recover and chase after me.

Thank goodness I had legs like my father.

After explaining all those things to Mama, I mentioned that the neighbor's doghouse needed a new coat of paint, trying to steer the bad news in a different direction. It didn't work. I could tell while I was talking that Mama was disappointed, although her expression hardly changed.

She put her fork down to note the seriousness of what she was about to say.

"I know you have difficulty with some of the other kids at school," she said, fixing her eyes on me with a sad smile, "especially when they make fun of the way you talk. But fighting is never the solution. Everyone should learn to be quick to listen, slow to speak, and slow to become angry. Let's try that next time."

I had the "slow to speak" part down, and all I could do was listen. The only part I needed lots of work on was the "slow to become angry." Just thinking about that made me mad.

I didn't even try to defend myself because the result would have been the same. The next day I had to go to Bobby's house to apologize for my anger management issues. I kept my focus on the hydrangea bush that overtook the front porch as I rang the doorbell. The chime set off a barking frenzy inside.

A muffled voice screamed, "Be quiet, Macho! Frank, someone's at the door. Macho, be quiet!"

Finally, the door opened.

"What do you want?" asked Mr. Wagner, peering through the unopened screen door while holding back a snarling Chihuahua with his foot.

"B-bb-bb—"

"I'll get Bobby for you," he said. "Bobby!" He yelled over his shoulder. "The little neighbor boy wants to see you."

I tensed in frustration at the fact that nobody ever let me finish a sentence. People just assumed what I was going to say. I could've been selling baked goods. For a split second, I thought about trying to sell Bobby some brownies, but I knew I'd never be able to pull off a stunt like that.

While we waited for Bobby, Mr. Wagner stood, unmoving, just inches in front of me. I stared down at his socks. They were baby blue and pulled to his knees. Macho yapped from behind Mr. Wagner's foot. I couldn't think of a more miserable punishment.

But then I peeked up just in time to see Bobby arrive with a bottom lip the size of a ripe melon. That made it all worth it.

However, stuttering out "I'm sorry" to Bobby and his father made minutes an eternity of torment. After I got out the last syllable, I turned and used my gift of running.

When I got home, I bypassed the living room to avoid Mama, who was reading a book, and ran to my room. I went straight to my desk and pulled out my journal. With tears in my eyes, I began to draw out each frame.

I turned the pencil on its edge and wrote the word *POW* in thick letters. I drew a squiggly line around the action. Johnny leveled Fred to the ground. Hero George swooped in with his cape still flowing in the air even after he'd landed.

"What have you done, Johnny?" Hero

George demanded. I erased and redrew his arms raised in question. The first time looked like he was caught in a stick up.

The stick figure of Johnny was a little thicker in the middle than usual. He held his hands up as if he were defeated. "I'm sorry, Hero George. Fred was mean to me."

Hero George hugged Johnny in an odd sort of fashion. "Is that the way to treat your friends? Haven't you heard of being slow to anger?" The bubble wasn't big enough to fit all the words, so they hung out the sides.

"I don't understand," Johnny said. "Nobody understands me. Why am I so different?"

Hero George stuck out his chest to look as though he were about to say something important. "Your difference is what makes you so special."

I stared at the page, slammed the book closed, and cried.

July 8, 1972: My Birthday

I didn't have many friends, and it wasn't because I made it a habit of hitting people. Another adult once explained to Mama that I kept an emotional distance from people as a means of protecting myself so I wouldn't get hurt. Who knew? All along I thought it was because I was shy and didn't like to talk to people.

Evidence that this well-meaning statement bothered Mama came out on my eighth birthday.

She was determined to give me the best party ever. She went all out with party favors, balloons, and an extra-fancy chocolate cake she'd brought home from the diner where she worked. She invited everyone I knew, but the only guest to show up was a boy named Willie, who was a year younger than me. I didn't really know him. He was the son of Mama's friend from bridge.

Willie handed a wrapped present to Mama and lay down by the front door to take off his shoes. He looked like a turtle stuck on its back. After he finished the grueling task, he stood, wiped off his hands, and said, "Hi, Badem. My name is Willie. I had to take a bath today."

Well, this was a promising start. Not that I wasn't grateful for his cleanliness, but I had no desire to dig into that statement. I looked at Mama with wide eyes, pleading for her to step in and help. She saw my need and moved into action.

"Why don't we take some pictures?" she said, motioning us together. She snapped a couple of pictures of us standing by the doorframe with the streamers and a happy birthday sign.

"Now you'll always have something to remember this day," she said, waving the Polaroid pictures in the air.

After they dried, she held them down for us to see. In one, Willie had his finger in his nose. In the other, I had my eyes closed. Perfect.

"Badem, let's play Pin the Tale on the

Donkey!" Willie's glasses slid down his nose, and when he pushed them back up, he snorted.

I gave Mama a sidelong glance. She made sure Willie wasn't looking—which wasn't difficult. He was spinning around in place, finger up his nose again. She mouthed, "Give him a chance. Everyone needs a friend, including him."

I knew she really meant me but let it slide.

In the first round, Willie nearly took out the lamp, the couch, and the coffee table. Mama had to stop spinning him around and, instead, positioned him right in front of the picture for him to get anywhere near it. When he pinned the tail on the donkey's ear, we declared him the winner. After six rounds I wasn't interested in playing anymore. The string on my party hat was digging unmercifully into my throat when Mama came to my rescue.

"Okay, boys, it's time for cake and ice cream. Then do you know what's next, *Babem*?" She overemphasized my name to correct Willie's mispronunciation, but it didn't work. "It's time for presents!"

Willie jumped up and down, mashing a wayward facedown tack from the donkey's tail into the carpet. "Oh boy, Badem, presents! I can't wait for you to unwrap mine."

I couldn't imagine what he'd gotten me.

Mama guided us into the kitchen where the table was spread with a plastic tablecloth and too many paper plates—she hadn't taken up the extras planned for the other invited guests. One lone present sat next to my cake. They were both positioned in front of a chair that had a green balloon rising above it. Willie bopped it when he raced by to get to the chair on the other side of me. Mama slid me closer to the table after I situated myself in the chair.

"Frank couldn't wait to make your cake again this year," she said. "He even added candy sprinkles on the sides. Do you like that?"

"Ye-y—" I stopped and nodded.

Talking in front of guests made me more uncomfortable than sitting in a bathtub full of dirty water. Thankfully Willie didn't mind talking. In fact, he never stopped. He was babbling something as he sat across from me, but I tuned him out.

Frank from the diner had made my birthday cake for the last four years, and this one was the best chocolate cake ever. He'd decorated it with a dog next to a fire hydrant. The red icing from the hydrant bled into the dog's white tail, turning it pink. I didn't mind. The inside was what mattered.

Willie sat on his knees and leaned closer to the cake. "Hey, I think that dog ate a whole pig. Look how fat he is in the middle!"

He was right. Frank wasn't an artist, but he didn't have to be. The cakes sold at the diner weren't decorated.

Willie filled his cheeks with air to demonstrate the dog's belly and then slapped them to make a pig-like noise. I laughed, and he repeated it.

"All right, boys, it's time to cut the cake, but we first have to sing." Mama winked at me as she lit the candles.

Before the party she'd asked permission to have a birthday song. Although I'd protested, she talked me into it. And this was it—she and Willie, an interesting pair. She counted to three, and together they sang an off-key duet that would've made a dog die from an overdose of pain. When it was over, she cut me a slice of cake larger than what I'd normally get. She even made sure to scrape the extra icing off the knife into a pile on my plate. With this, I forgave the humiliation.

"Willie, do you mind getting an end piece?" she asked, already balancing it over his plate.

"That's great!" Willie said. "I like chocolate. That's my favorite. My mom thinks I like carrot cake. I'm not sure why. The first time I had it, I threw up. But that's what she makes me every year for my birthday." He shook his head, causing his glasses to nearly fall into his milk. He shoved them back up and snorted.

The cake was so good I tolerated Willie's slurping noises as he gobbled up the lumpy stew-like mixture he'd made by chopping up the cake and stirring it together with the melted ice cream. Oddly enough, even with the combination of the two, it took him twice as long to eat it. I was glad when it was finally time for my present.

"I think you'll like what I got you," Willie said, handing me a rectangular gift wrapped in a brown paper bag. "I like it."

That was what I was afraid of.

I timidly took it and smiled to look eager. It didn't look like anything special, but as I unwrapped it, I grew more excited with each tear. I quickly uncovered a box that pictured a boy holding a white plane with a blue stripe painted on the side. The model airplane was perfect. I'd always wanted one.

"Th-th-th-than-thank ya-ya-yo-you," I said, half-expecting some kind of a joke about my speech.

Not from Willie.

"You're welcome, Badem," he said, sliding his arm across his runny nose. "I really like that name. Badem. It sounds like an action figure's name. Like someone who can conquer any bad guy around." He did a few karate moves. "Mine's just Willie. It doesn't sound like I could hurt even a flower. My grandmother was the one who came up with my name when she saw how pink I was when I was a baby. Whatever that means."

As I watched Willie begin to run laps around the living room, I realized I didn't have the heart to tell him that Badem wasn't my name. It became my nickname. Even Mama used it at times.

Willie paused in his sprint to karate chop the armchair. "Thanks for inviting me to your party," he said. "It's been fun. My grandparents are the only ones invited to my parties. They just sit around and talk about their bunions and how expensive everything is. This is much better. Maybe you can come to my party in a couple of months." He pushed his glasses back up his nose and snorted. "Do you want to put the plane together now? I've done four—only one, though, without the help of my dad. The wings were lopsided and the propeller fell off, but it still looked cool."

We worked on it together, Willie chattering all the while. Mama snapped a few more pictures of the two of us holding the half-completed plane, and that time, they turned out great. Willie left with a promise to come over again soon to paint the plane.

Mama had succeeded. That was the best party ever.

That night I went upstairs and set the plane on my desk. I admired it awhile before taking out my journal and beginning my entry. The *Hero George* cartoon flowed out of me.

Hero George strutted in with a friend. "Hello, Johnny, I want you to meet someone."

I tried drawing a kid with glasses, but he turned out looking like a burglar.

"This is Victor," Hero George said in the next

frame. "You will like him a lot."

I drew Johnny's eyebrows slanted in anger. "NO!"

The saddest look crossed Hero George's face. "But, Johnny, everyone needs a friend."

In the last frame, I drew Johnny and Victor giving each other awkward high fives.

October 24, 1973: Dad's Leaving

If I could have predicted those definable moments that gave me no choice of my own, I would have never stopped running from them.

"Your dad's not coming back," Mama said, curling up on the sofa next to me and pulling the afghan over her legs. She'd brought me a cup of hot cocoa with a blob of peppermint chocolate melted on top as an offering of comfort.

It wasn't comfort enough. Sitting on my knees with my head propped on the back of the couch, I stared out the window at the soggy landscape. The pane was still christened with condensation, and the driveway was wiped clean of the dirt Willie and I had piled on it to make a fort. It took us two hours after school to dig and haul dirt to get it perfect, and we were only able to play in it for thirty minutes before Willie's dad came to pick him up. That was the day before, and what seemed a lifetime ago. I tried to keep my mind in that moment, not wanting to or simply not knowing how to respond to Mama's comment.

A voice inside me was yelling, but it couldn't get past the emptiness to escape.

My dad had left for Memphis a month ago. With each passing day, I tried to make excuses as to where he could be and told myself that he always left but always came back. But nothing could cover the ache that formed in my heart, and after a couple of weeks, I knew deep down he wouldn't be coming home.

"You know it's not your fault, right?" Mama tried one more time to offer me the mug, and I just stared at it.

It had to be my fault. Dad wanted a normal boy, one that wasn't timid and awkward, and one he could relate to. I'd heard him and Mama fighting on several occasions about how he never spent time with me. The bottom line was that he didn't know how to talk to me.

I'd wanted to share my *Hero George* cartoons with him. He liked to draw, so I knew he'd like them. I never got the chance.

"Sweetheart, it had nothing to do with you," Mama said, pulling me from my thoughts. She put the hot cocoa on the coffee table. "He met someone else while he was away on business, and he fell in love with her. That type of love does strange things to people."

Maybe I was too young to understand the different types of love. But what I did know was that the love he was supposed to have had for us was a special kind that shouldn't have been shared. It wasn't a multiplying love like when someone gets a new brother or sister. The parents would say there would be enough love to go around. No. The love for us was supposed to have been a singular kind, meant only for us. If any amount was given to anybody else, then there was less for us.

"I-I don-don't un-un-der-st-stand th-at l-love."

"It's hard to explain." Mama's look went distant. "I guess it's really just selfishness, which isn't actually love. That's why you don't understand it. It likes to mimic love—that's why people get caught up in it. But it's false. True love, on the other hand, conquers all." She kissed my forehead. "And that's what kind of love I have for you."

Hurt filled the void that the selfish love left behind. My bottled-up tears shook my body until I dry-heaved them up. I collapsed into Mama's arms and let her hold me well into the night. When she thought I was asleep, Mama carried me upstairs and tucked me into bed. After she shut the door, I crept to my desk and brought my journal back to the bed.

I drew only one frame. Hero George held Johnny while he cried. The dialogue bubble said, "Help me to know true love." A tear fell on top of the picture, crumpling the page well after the wetness dried.

May 11, 1974: Painful Advice

The gurgle of the fish tank masked the receptionist's typing. A blue and red fish swam by my nose as I watched the bubbles rise from the coral. Just as I sat back in the uncomfortable chair, a man who tried to cover his baldness with a swoop of thin hair walked out of the side door.

He held up a chart and said, "Babem Oxenbow?"

"H-h-here," I said like it was roll call at school.

"Come, follow me." He turned on his heels and briskly walked away, assuming I was behind him.

I left the Narnia book I hadn't read on the chair and quickly caught up. When we got to his office, he motioned for me to sit on a big black couch. He took a seat in the chair opposite me.

"Now, Mr. Oxenbow, it says here that your mother feels as though you're depressed. Would you care to explain?"

That was a depressing question. It took me at least the next ten minutes to fumble out the fact that I wasn't exactly sure what he meant by that. Finally, the doctor handed me a piece of paper and asked me to write out why I thought I was there. I was pretty sure my sigh of relief was audible. I took the paper and addressed the situation the best way I knew how.

Dear Doctor, I can't talk. My daddy left me, and the kids at school still make fun of me. Babem.

That about summed up my life.

That must've done it, because the doctor spent the next forty-five minutes doing the talking. I didn't understand most of what he had to say, but one of his metaphors did stick. He said my life was like a runaway locomotive. All I'd done was stand cold in my tracks and let it plow me down. He told me I needed to learn to jump on top of it and ride out the storm. It would be a little bumpy at first but would hurt less that way.

We paid a lot of money for him to tell me that, so I wanted to act as though I understood. I did a lot of nodding. Afterward, I fished around in a bowl and got a plastic spider ring I knew Mama would throw out the first time I wasn't looking. Thank goodness Willie was there to explain everything to me when I got home.

"Ah, Badem, it's simple," Willie said after I told him the doctor's philosophy. "I'll demonstrate what it means. Stand right here. I'll pull the wagon up with me, and when I come down, you hop in."

I shrugged. It seemed innocent enough.

Willie teetered off on his newest bicycle. His dad was a dentist and always bought him the latest models. I'd scored his old one five months before.

While Willie pedaled up Yam Hill and

positioned himself at the top, I spotted Mr. Hobblenick watering his flowers. I liked the Hobblenicks. His wife made the best apple pies and always gave me a slice whenever she baked them for her senior citizens club at church. I smiled and waved at Mr. Hobblenick. As he waved back, I caught the brunt of the impact from Willie's demonstration. With his brakes screeching, Willie skidded to the left, and I went flying into the mailbox. The accident required five stitches in my chin and a cast for my broken leg.

Yep, the doctor was right. My life definitely felt like I was being run over by a runaway train— or at least a runaway bike. Never again would I just stand there and let life plow me over. But I liked Mama's insight better. Not to mention it was a lot less painful.

"Babem," she said as she propped my broken leg onto a stack of pillows. "I know you feel overwhelmed by life and question why things are the way they are. But I want you to understand one thing. The hardest circumstances can turn into the greatest blessings. Sometimes it just takes a little time."

Along with a bowl of ice cream, she brought my journal to me while I sat on the couch. I used a purple crayon for Victor's bike because I needed to sharpen the blue one. It was hard drawing Johnny with a broken leg. I slurped up the rest of the ice cream and concentrated again on the cast.

Finally I got to the last frame. Hero George stood beside Johnny with a hand on his shoulder and said, "Don't worry, Johnny. Everything will turn out okay."

December 14, 1975: My Purpose

I wasn't sure how much time bad things needed in order to morph into something good, but during the church's Christmas pageant the following year, I began to get a taste of what Mama meant.

The Christmas pageant was pretty predictable. I was always one of the sheep. It was one of those special parts that didn't require any tryouts. My instructions were to sit there and say nothing. Foolproof. I even had my own costume they pulled from the closet every year and glued back on any cotton balls that had fallen off during storage.

Priscilla, the girl I liked, was usually Mary, and Howard, a ninny, was always Joseph. Ms. Garrett, the director, insisted on having a live donkey every year to carry Priscilla down the aisle. The kids liked it because it always pooped on stage and made us laugh. We paid the janitor overtime to stay and clean it up during the performance. He wore black to blend in during the scene changes, but he was still noticeable.

During the Christmas pageant of 1975, everything went awry.

When Ms. Garrett arrived at the church, the gate to the donkey's pen was wide open, and the donkey was nowhere in sight. Hours of searching left the crew still empty-handed. We found out three days later that a fraternity had played a prank on us by hiding the donkey in their basement, but that didn't help us in the moment.

"What are we going to do?" Ms. Garrett asked in a panic to her assistant, Maude.

I happened to be standing there, putting on my sheep costume. It was getting a little snug. Time for more fabric. Maude looked around the crowded room until her eyes fell on me. I felt exposed.

"Why not use Babem as the donkey?" she asked. "We already have two other sheep."

I stopped mid-dress to calm my beating heart. It was sad to get excited about being a donkey, but it felt like a promotion. The perk was I'd get to carry Priscilla on my back. I would've been a skunk for that.

Ms. Garrett stared at me from above her glasses. As others donned their costumes, it was as if everything moved in slow motion.

"Can you handle that, Babem?" she finally asked, sounding greatly annoyed.

I nodded, hoping not to give away my enthusiasm.

"Fine, you can be the donkey. All you have to do is carry Priscilla down the aisle and sit there when she gets off your back. Nothing more. The janitor will be glad for a relaxing evening for once. Maude, go get the cow costume from the barnyard production and makeshift it into a donkey. Cut some donkey ears out of construction paper and put them on a headband. That should be good enough for tonight. Hurry, the play starts in forty-five minutes."

If that were the only problem that happened, then I would have only been known as the real donkey's replacement. But the pieces fell into place for my big moment. Howard's mom soon stepped in to add the sweet frosting on the cake.

"Ms. Garrett?" Howard's mom said, cowering by the door. She clutched her purse to her stomach as if trying to use it as an antacid.

Ms. Garrett was stooped over a girl, safety pinning angel wings to her back. She halfway glanced up. Three more pins dangled from her mouth.

"Howard has laryngitis."

The pins fell to the floor. The air was sucked dry of every shout, murmur, and snicker. Gary, our backup Joseph, who had thought he was just going to be the innkeeper because we'd never had to use our backup Joseph, fainted and fell on top of the cardboard inn, knocking it over, causing a domino effect of cardboard chaos.

The shouts and screams that came afterward may not have been controlled if it weren't for the strength of Ms. Garrett's voice. "Silence!" she said as she jumped onto a folding chair to regain our attention.

Everyone froze in place. The last cardboard house dropped next to my feet, but I was too afraid to acknowledge it.

"Someone wake up Gary and get a beard on him, and then get the inn, houses, and manger back up and ready to be carried out." Ms. Garrett raised her arms above her head, making her look like a frenzied gorilla. "We're not stopping the show now!"

It may have been out of sheer fear, but that command set everything into motion. By the time Ms. Garrett played the first note on the piano, we were all positioned and ready. It didn't matter that Gary's beard was lopsided or that I looked like a cow unsuccessfully trying to pass itself off as a donkey. The show was going to happen.

After a few dancing snowmen and a group singing on a sleigh (I never understood how that fit into the nativity story), my part came. All the lights went out except for a single spotlight on Priscilla and me. Gary walked beside us, but I didn't give him a thought.

I struggled to get Priscilla down the aisle. It was easier imagining it than actually doing it. The beach ball shoved under her robe must've been filled with a hundred pounds' worth of pellets, because there was no way such a petite girl could have been so heavy. Not to mention the bulkiness of the costume kept tripping me up.

"Why is that cow shaking?" a little girl whispered to her dad when I teetered by.

"I think it's supposed to be a donkey," he whispered back. "He's having a little trouble carrying the girl."

Yes, I was, and by the time I climbed the altar steps on all fours, I'd broken a sweat and nearly collapsed. I never thought I would be so thankful to get Priscilla off my back. During the next few scenes, I recuperated. The twitch that had started in my left leg finally stopped.

By this time, Gary had grown deathly pale. He stumbled through his lines while Maude hid behind the risers to guide him. Like a reverse echo, the whisper came first with the booming voice following in trembling waves.

When the new innkeeper shouted his line, "There's no room in the inn," the music started. It was time for Joseph and Mary's duet. Ms. Garrett had written a new song this year for the part. I had it memorized, singing it in my head a thousand times while I dreamed of performing alongside Priscilla. I listened with my eyes closed, careful not to sway. Priscilla began singing her part. She had a voice like an angel—not like Mary Ruth, the second angel to the right, who sounded like she was caught in a stampede, but like I thought a real angel would sound.

When Joseph's part came, Gary didn't sing. I peeked. He stared blankly at the crowd with his beard pointed toward the piano. Priscilla kept going, while encouraging him to join her with wide, shifting eyes. It didn't happen. That was when my will took over and made me do something I would have never done if I'd reasonably thought it through.

I jumped up, not thinking of how it looked to have a cow-donkey pop up from the background, and started to sing. I began timidly at first, until I discovered that the words flowed from my mouth without laboring over them. That was something I'd never experienced before. As I flawlessly sang along, confidence came from the unhindered strength of my voice. Hooves and all, I extended my arms and tilted my head back to embrace the richness of the moment. I was free. Every note came as perfectly as I thought them, and I soared to a height I'd never gone before. Though Priscilla was stunned, she didn't miss a beat. It made her only more powerful.

And together we sang.

Ms. Garrett's mouth fell open, Maude peeked from behind the risers, and every kid stood still on stage. Two rows from the front, I could see tears in Mama's eyes. Willie, who sat next to her, gave me a thumbs-up.

As we sang the final words—"Who has room for our baby boy?"—I wanted to hang on to the fading notes. I did so for as long as I could until the lights dimmed for the next scene. I bowed my head to absorb the remaining moments with my body numbing as it warded off the overdose of adrenaline. It was then that the crowd erupted into applause.

The only light that came on was from the star above the manger. Its faint yet all-encompassing glow lit the audience's faces. Ms. Garrett stood to her feet with the rest rising behind her. Maude came from the shadows, and Mama and Willie hollered as loud as they could.

Baby Jesus might've been born that night, but God allowed another miracle—I found my voice.

"You did it, Babem!" Mama shouted as she hugged me too tight after the program.

Willie found my head, which was being sandwiched between Mama's arms. "Way to go, Badem," he said. "I can't wait to hear more of your voice. You sing. I'll just talk. You don't want me to sing. My mom says that God gave me lots of gifts; singing just isn't one of them. We have lots to talk about."

Mama stopped hugging me but held me at arms' length. "You can sing! What a wonderful purpose you have. Let's go and celebrate."

Later that night, the sheet covered my head and the flashlight blinked with its low battery as I stayed up hours after the party, drawing the *Hero*

George cartoon. It was a celebration of Johnny, who was learning to be a hero himself.

Hero George wrapped a cape that was too long around Johnny's shoulders. "You did it, Johnny! Now you know your purpose."

I turned off the light and had the best night's sleep ever.

November 27, 2017: Saying Goodbye to a Hero

I flip back through the worn pages of the journal. Each memory conjures up another emotion. For the last time, I pick up a pencil. I draw out Johnny singing for kings and queens, movie stars, and presidents. But the last frame is the most important. Hero George is in the hospital bed and asks Johnny to sing for him.

As the notes fill the room, Hero George says, "I couldn't be more proud of who you turned out to be. God had to shape you in order for you to be the best you could be."

"It's time to go, honey," Priscilla, my wife, says as she interrupts my thoughts.

I slip the journal into my pocket and head to the graveside service. Willie is the pastor—only God could use his gift of incessant talking for a greater good. He greets our family and leads us to where our closest friends and family are gathered. After the final words are said, Willie allows me to be alone with Mama one last time before she's lowered into the ground.

I pull out the journal. "M-m-mama," I say with tears streaming down my face, "Th-this is f-for y-ya-you. Th-this is h-how I s-saw my l-life, b-b-but thr-through y-your eyes, y-you al-ways s-saw m-me as hav-having a gr-great-er pur-purpose."

I close my eyes and say a prayer, thanking God for giving me a mother who believed that I had a purpose beyond how others or I saw myself. Then I place my worn journal on top of all the flowers. The final page blows open, revealing the last words I've written to her: *To Mom, the greatest hero a boy could ever have. Love, Babem.*

CHAPTER 5

Out of the Author's Journal

Part 2

♫

I'm grateful I encountered a loving God at an early age. At the same time, in my own life, I've been damaged through words, crushed by legalism, and judged with hypocritical statements. This is all from people who profess to be Christians. Unfortunately this is what I often see happening in the world. So many people have a warped idea of God because of the people they encounter, the events happening around them, and the experiences they have. That's understandable, but that also breaks my heart. The Church has a beautiful message of hope that is often missed by those who so desperately need it, all because of our own selfish pride.

When I try to walk in the shoes of others and understand what they're going through, I often fail miserably. But I still try to put myself in their place. I've had my own experiences that have left me reeling in disbelief. Again, I took to writing out my confusion as I tried to interpret the God I know against the pain I saw in the world. Here's a glimpse of my journey that has played out in my journal:

♫

My husband and I, along with our two boys, stood in the castle's chapel. On the walls were neatly painted verses from the book of Psalms that told the truth of God's majesty and glory. In a ghostly setting of yesteryear, the chairs were set in rows as if still waiting in anticipation for the next service to begin, and the empty pulpit told of the sermons that once had been spoken from it. Dust had long settled over the room, shrouding it in an eerie overtone of death. What should have been a celebration of people from the past, gathering to worship a great and awesome God, instead was an overwhelming sense of sorrow that deeply grieved me.

Right beneath our feet, in this Ghanaian castle, were the dungeons where the female slaves had been kept. Human beings, created by God, were herded into small, overcrowded chambers and left there until the ships docked. Then they were forced to leave their homeland through the Door of No Return. In kidnapping raids throughout villages, husbands and wives were ripped from each other, and many parents never saw their children again. They were stripped of their humanity, only to be given the value of property meant for someone else's gain.

The reality of their pain that had happened so long ago became a distant thought loosely captured by an old structure displaying a remnant of the past. Try as it might, the slave castle could give only a small picture of the ugly it had experienced. Without the characters that embodied the stories, the noises that spoke of the heartache, or the putrid smells that took away all human dignity, it failed to fully deliver the impact of such an atrocity. So all I could do was stand inside the four walls of the chapel and imagine the wails of lament coming from the mouths of those women who, in just one instant, lost everything. Their sobs rising through the rafters to intermingle with the hymns of praise to God must have produced a mournful, contradictory sound. Both grieved the heart of God, just not in the same way.

What an impact that one room made on my life. That paradox of sorrow and praise—and everything else that went along with it—should have never been written into the pages of history. But it was, and those tragic moments that can never be erased have buried themselves into memories. Even with the triumph of freedom that broke the curse of slavery, the lingering ignorance still clings in the form of racism. Again, I've wept in agonizing shame at the Church's response to an issue that was born out of superiority, dominance, and fear. Unfortunately racism has hit much closer to home for me than that castle in Ghana.

I grew up in the southern part of the United States as a white female in a middle-class, Christian home. I confess that one sentence alone can make people laugh at the fact that racism has ever touched me on a personal level, and they would be right in the sense that I can't fully grasp the lives of those with stereotypes and targets on their backs because of being born with a particular color of skin. I won't even try to say that I remotely know what that's like, but I've observed with my eyes and listened with my heart to try to grasp the impact that it's had on people.

In 1979, I began kindergarten and was able to sit in the classroom next to people of different colors and cultures. That's not really surprising because segregation supposedly ended in 1958. However, at the age of five, I knew nothing about Ruby Bridges or the brave men and women who fought for equal rights in our country and paved the way for my own experiences in school. All I knew was that I had friends who were different. What I had trouble comprehending at such a young age was why people had such anger toward them. I had to be taught that their differences made them beneath me. Maybe I'm just a slow learner, but I still don't get it.

I grew up in Stone Mountain, Georgia, which is considered the modern birthplace of the Ku Klux Klan. I remember going into town on Saturday mornings with my parents and seeing the men dressed in their white robes and ghostly hoods. Although these men weren't directing their slander or throwing rocks at my family because of our white privilege, I still feared them and hid on the floorboard of our car so I wouldn't be seen. I had irrational fears that I would wake up to a cross burning in our yard because someone would find out my inner thoughts that people of color really were all right.

When my family moved to Mississippi, the atmosphere wasn't really any different. In the deep south of the Bible belt, we'd sing songs in Sunday school about Jesus loving all the little children of the world—"red and yellow, black and white, they are precious in his sight"—yet the Church as a whole was seen as a vehicle of hate toward any kind of difference. Although my immediate family never used derogatory slander toward anyone of a different color or race, those words were all around me. People sat in churches for the sake of tradition, yet hate seemed more engrained in people than the Word of God. When I grew older, I even realized that people from the church I grew up in had been part of the KKK that fueled the next generation to hate, becoming the echoes from the past that can still be heard today.

Watching racism play out in my own life and standing in a slave castle at the root of where such bigotry began, I saw where the Church has stood so many times on the wrong side of issues. Out of one side of our mouths we sing praises to God, while out of the other side, we slander the ones we're commanded to love. The present legacies defining the Church to the world today are the stories about parents who've abandoned their children when they come out as LGBT, people dressing as the grim reaper and picketing abortion clinics, or the continuing saga of sex scandals riddling the Church. The list goes on. What distresses me the most is that none of these things reflect the beauty of God's character. What people are witnessing is a human antidote to a messed-up world. And nobody wants to swallow that bitter pill.

My point isn't to rant about the Church and how bad it is. In fact, it's quite the opposite. As a pastor's wife, I understand that the Church is the bride of Christ and has been commanded to make disciples of all nations as we reflect God's glory to others. Praise God, there are many churches that do exactly that. These churches are the voices who sing the love song to a world that so desperately needs to hear it over the noise.

I can apologize to a hurting world for all the wrongs of spiritual abuse, but I can't correct what has happened with just a few short stories. My own heart was won over through example after loving example that helped me encounter a God who takes great joy and delight in me. I hope the same for you. I want to open up my journal in the hope that, through the world of fiction, you'll see my characters wrestle with the mess of ugliness and triumph in a world that doesn't make sense.

CHAPTER 6

Color of Redemption

♫

"I've seen a man die."

The creak of the front-porch swing blended with the song of the cicadas, while Grandma continued to snap peas and gently sway it back and forth with her toes as if she'd just mentioned the setting sun. I stopped rocking in my chair. And waited. No longer aware of the lulling time. My mama once told me Grandma had a secret, but I'd never ventured a guess as to what it was.

"Over yonder." Grandma's gaze fell past the rows of pecan trees lining her acreage. "You know that lone oak tree, Nora Rae, the one standing next to the Johnsons' property?"

It was too dark to see it now, but I knew which one she meant. I'd spent many summers climbing its branches and swinging beneath its canopy on the old tire swing now gone. Grandma popped a pea into her mouth and chewed really slow. Her gaze turned vacant, but her hands kept the pace with each pod: picking, peeling, sliding—moving to their own steady beat.

"That's right where he died." Her jaw set taut before she swallowed. "Hung underneath, he was."

Despite the heat, the thought turned me cold.

Grandma started humming as she picked up a dish towel and dabbed her face. The strains of "Amazing Grace" were suspended midair by heavy drops of humidity, and each note reached my ear in a muffled drawl. She fanned out the towel and blotted the back of her neck as the song rose in intensity. The night air was stitched together by the tune, but when she put the towel down, her humming ceased. The drone of the box fan filled the void.

"I watched from the old barn that sat right up there on that hill, I did." She tilted her head in a vague direction. "Perfect spot, too. Nobody knew I was there . . . nobody, that is, 'cept him."

Condensation slid from my glass of lemonade and onto my hand, jolting me with its sudden tickle. I dared not to brush it off.

"Yep, every town has its secrets."

Grandma shifted the peas in the bowl and plucked out a few bad ones. One pea tumbled over the side, rolled past my feet, and slipped through the wooden slats into the darkness below.

"If you catch the right person and give them your ear, they'll fill it full of stories about the Xavier Praxton murder. Heard of it?"

1941. Xavier Praxton, a white pastor, was brutally attacked and killed by a colored man. The colored man was chased down by several local men and hanged, making news clear past West Feliciana Parish.

"I've heard of it." My tone told my judgment. "Mrs. Danes said that man had it coming to him."

"Mm, hmm . . . everyone owns their opinions, I 'spose," said Grandma. "But ain't nobody around here who knows the real story."

She put a pod between her teeth, pulled it through, and tossed aside the empty hull. A grunt rolled in the back of her throat as she shook her head.

"No ma'am, they wouldn't know, 'cause it's a secret," she declared.

A wayward mosquito buzzed by Grandma's arm, and she killed it first swat. When she wiped the remains on her apron, my eyes fixed on the jagged scar across the back of her hand— "Schoolyard injury, roughing it with too many boys," she always told me as to how she got it. She caught my gawk, and I averted my eyes down to my sneakers, though I could still feel her gaze on me.

"I ain't never gotten the colored man's image out of my head." Grandma's voice rose, competing with the nearby bullfrogs. "Calm, he was. Calmer than a man should be 'fore his death. When he looked my way, he never flinched. He stood tall, straight up like a beanpole, staring his coal eyes up at me. And at the last second, he raised up his chin, as a man would do if he were 'bout to die a respectable death. I'll never forget his gurgling gasps, the last one sealing all secrets within him."

I couldn't look up. An ant weaved in and out of the wooden spindles, while sadness, pain, and confusion broke Grandma's voice.

"I ran."

I squeezed my eyes shut.

"But the blood followed me—on my feet, on my hands, on my Sunday best. My feet beat so hard against the gravel road that it turned to dust. I could have sworn my knees were going to pound a hollow right through my chest. I cut across the field, down into the forest, and stopped only when I got to Pepper Creek. That's when I tried to scream out what I had seen, what I felt. With every wail and every holler, the voice inside me fought hard to get out. But words failed me. They got stuck before my lips. No ma'am, I couldn't say anything. Not at all. It was a secret."

Grandma stopped the swing, and all of nature caught its breath. I peeked, scared to look, but saw her eyes, too, were closed. A bead of sweat fought to get through the maze of creases on her forehead. Then, as if knowing I was staring, she opened her eyes and held my gaze.

"Do you tell secrets?" Grandma asked.

I started to answer, but Grandma kept going, lost in another world.

"That's what he always asked me after putting his finger over my lips, locking them tight, and throwing away the key."

It was the way Grandma said it, the slight hiss in her words. I knew she no longer spoke of the colored man on that tree. I couldn't swallow, but somehow a line of saliva eased its way down the back of my throat.

"He always called me pretty, that he did, whispering it to me with the rhythm of his body — "You're a pretty girl, such a pretty girl." But instead, he made me feel like I was downright ugly and full of filth. When he'd had his way with me, he'd put his clothes back on, spit on me, and curse me for making him sin." Grandma stopped and heaved her belly well past her chest before letting it fall with a sigh.

The silence held thick. A spark of a firefly glinted life to me, then another further off in the distance. It was the only creature brave enough to intrude. Perhaps it knew it was the only thing that could relieve the darkness.

"He made his weekly visits to our house long past three years; sometimes he came twice a week if there were special occasions he needed tending to. Special occasions?" Grandma snorted a laugh I felt down to my toes. "Mother thought visiting so often was something a good preacher man would do, oh yes. But she wasn't to blame. No. I don't 'spect she ever knew. I never told anyone, not one soul. That was my secret."

She chewed off the end of a pod and spit it right back out.

"But when I turned nine, I'd had enough. It was going to be his last visit; I'd make sure of that. Yes ma'am, I'd make sure of that." Grandma emphasized the last words with a slight nod of her head.

My hand grew numb from its grip around the arm of the rocker. The water that had collected from the earlier shower trickled off the eaves into an upturned bucket, one lone drop at a time; each *plit* counted away the slow country seconds. After the torment of reflective silence, she began again.

"When no one was looking, I stole the same knife they used to cut my birthday cake." Grandma pursed her lips as her hands tore at a snap pea. "I knew Pastor Praxton would take the shortcut across Mr. Riley's field like he always did, and this time, I decided to follow. The stars shone so bright that night I thought for sure they were hung there just to give me away. Oh, I can't tell you how many times I almost lost my courage; I would have, too, if it weren't for the gnawing chill that took over my body, urging me forward."

Grandma's hands tensed so tightly around the rim of the bowl her fingers almost disappeared. When the breeze blew, it was sterile. I was afraid of breathing it in.

"I hadn't thought of any plan. Didn't know I was 'sposed to. It was only when Pastor Praxton got to the back side of the mill that I gathered enough nerve to approach him. But that's when he heard me. As he turned around, I ran so furiously at him, hands up, knife out, I didn't give him much time to respond. With every jab, I yelled at him, crying out that forbidden secret with every stroke. It had to come out, or I was going to be the one that died. But I was already dying inside from those slow, whispering taunts of disgrace. What else could I have done?" She bit back a tear and looked sternly at me.

I wasn't meant to answer.

"He was long dead 'fore I stopped. Some say he was stabbed in thirty-seven different places, but I'd honestly lost count. Didn't care. When I was finished, I laid down the knife, stumbled backward, and fell down from exhaustion. Tears came to me only as an afterthought. And that, Nora Rae, is when I felt him standing above me."

I felt his presence through the intensity of her words and shivered. Grandma soundlessly put the bowl beside her and gathered her apron into her fists, and I tensed with her. Only the forward creak of the rocking chair broke the dusk heat as

I leaned forward.

"I knew I was in trouble. I'd done something only thoughts allow you to do. I huddled there trembling, not wanting to look up. So I stared hard at his worn sneakers and tried to wish my way into a dream. Voices from a distance drew close as men from the mill changed shifts. Fear turned my tears into a burning punishment. Then something happened."

Grandma paused to wipe her eyes with the corner of her apron. Anxiety wrung me with its unmerciful grasp, twisting my stomach.

"Hands, darker than soot, reached down and took hold of my shoulders. I was expecting to be yanked up, scolded, and handed over in shame. But that's not what happened. No ma'am. After bringing me to my feet, this man stooped low and picked up the knife that reeked of my deed. My feet were rooted in confusion as I wondered what he was going to do. I wanted to get away, I did. But there was nowhere to run.

"As the voices grew louder, he looked me straight in the eyes and spoke real soft." Grandma slid to the edge of the swing and leaned so close to me that the sting of her breath tickled my cheek. "Do you want to know what he said?"

I barely nodded.

"He said, 'Your secret's been told; it's safe with me. Now go on. I'll take the blame.'"

Grandma spoke so hushed I nearly missed

what she'd said. But even if she'd talked to me like we were out on a picnic by the old gristmill, I still would've second guessed if I'd heard correctly.

"I didn't know what to do," Grandma said. "The voices had already reached the corner. I shook my head and tried to speak, but only one word came out—'Why?' That's all I wanted to know. However, the men from the mill appeared 'fore he was given the chance to answer. He just shoved me into the shadows. When the men saw the preacher's body next to a colored man with a bloody knife, they took off after him and never bothered to ask any questions. Of course, that man knew that was exactly what they'd do. That's how things were done back then. Uh, huh. Sad, but true."

Confusion ate me whole. I wanted to know why he'd do such a thing. No one would ever trade life for certain death.

Grandma slowly rose, placed the bowl under her arm, and shuffled to the door. The light from inside filtered through the door's mesh, forming a crisscross pattern across her face. It framed the woman who'd stayed so strong for Mama and me over the past six months in a tarnished glow.

Grandma opened the door and propped it against her back. "What's love, Nora Rae?"

The millions of ways to answer fell flat, so I held my tongue.

"I never knew it," she said. "Not back then.

That concept was stolen from me over some man's lust. Sure was. Now I've had long years to think about that day when I watched that colored man die; yes, I have. I'd always wanted to know that answer. Why? Why'd anyone do such a thing?"

Looking up toward the porch light, she leaned against the door and then shook her head. The armor I'd seen Grandma wear was dented with a tear. It caught just the corner of her eye and glistened in the light. I could tell she wrestled with that thought.

"Do you want to know why he did it?" she asked.

I knew she'd tell me.

"Now, of course, Pastor Praxton shouldn't have died like that. Well, I should say that it wasn't for my hands to act as judge. I'm certain that colored man knew that too. But it wasn't about all that. That man knew the guilt I bore was too much for me to bear. I shouldn't have gone through what I did. No one should've. But in that one moment, his act redefined my understanding of love. He knew the power of what that'd do to me and was willing to sacrifice everything for me to catch a glimpse of true love. That's what he did for me. Its effect has lasted long past that one day. Now I'd do everything for you to understand that kind of love."

Before she turned to walk inside, I said, "Grandma."

Grandma waited in stilled composure for my words.

I knew why she'd told me her secret. I'd been in a world of hurt over the past few months. Everything I'd ever known had changed.

I took a breath and asked, "Is that why you took us in after Daddy left us?"

She gave me a hint of a smile, just enough to let me know that she understood. "No child should have love defined for her by an ugly world. I'll do whatever it takes to let you know that."

As Grandma walked inside, the screen door banged shut behind her. The strains of "Amazing Grace" filled the air once again, embracing me with the fullness of its sound.

CHAPTER 7

As You Love Me

♫

The song struck a chord so low even darkness bent its ear to listen. The southern air, steeped in sorrow's grief, dripped its humid tears down leaves, stalks, and blades, while the moon reflected a shadowed dance in response to the melody. Fields bowed their bolls. Wisps of cotton idled without breath. Kwame's pain, pronounced with such articulate grace, shaped the heavens' forlorn face.

On the night Kwame sang, his voice was the only thing man couldn't shackle. Years later, I can look back and see the gift he gave to us. Its truth is still buried deep within my heart. And it's become part of my story—one I have to tell.

I first knew Kwame as a legend, a ghost who blended into the eaves of the plantation where I grew up. Every Friday night the community would gather on our front porch and sip iced tea and tell stories. Most of the stories were just gossip about who was now with whom and what was happening with each family; the drone of it all usually put me to sleep right in Mama's arms.

But anyone who began to share about a chance encounter with Kwame immediately had everyone's full focus, including mine. Pastor Edmund was the one who drew our attention the most. He'd often find Kwame nestled in the church's bell tower and would have to shoo him away. "Clearing out the demons" was how the deacons referred to this act.

The biggest uproar came when Pastor Edmund told us he'd discovered Kwame surrounded by piles of jagged pictures—Kwame had torn all the illustrations out of the church's Bibles. Normally I didn't get too upset with Kwame, because nothing he did really pertained to me. But that one frustrated me. The pictures were the only things I understood in the Bible. I'd stare at them during the long, drawn out sermons and think about what life would be like in the different scenes.

I was excited when we held a church fund drive to replace the ruined Bibles. The ceremony was a big to-do. One highlight was the Cleaver family being praised for giving the biggest donation—they got to cut the ribbon off the crate. But when I opened the first new Bible, my excitement fell. The only pictures I saw were maps. I wasn't sure who would want that.

But that was probably the point. They did everything they could to keep Kwame from tearing them up again. After the deacons boarded up the loose siding and put the new Scriptures under lock and key, not a single page went missing.

To most, Kwame was a pastime, someone used as a spice to add excitement to our boring lives. But I found out he was something more. We all did.

The night it happened, I stood by my bedroom window, trying to feel any kind of a breeze on the hot, summer evening. But the stale air just wouldn't circulate. Dusk's warmth didn't play fair as it smothered any kind of stirring.

"Lily Ann!" Mama's voice preceded her hurried entry into the bedroom.

Her tone was sharp, but it wasn't to scold me. I hadn't done anything wrong. However, nothing was right. I'd felt it. The day was packed with the added chores of getting everything prepared for the big event. Everyone was on edge, including me, though I'd nothing to do with anything— except for maybe getting in the way.

"I want you to stay put in your room, you hear?" she instructed.

I nodded while picking at the sore on my elbow.

"Are you all right?" She walked farther into the room and squatted in front of me. She took my hands into hers, probably to keep me from pulling off the already loose scab.

"Everything's going to be okay, you hear? There's nothing for you to worry about. Look at me."

I lifted my head. Her normally fresh face was streaked with sweat, and she hadn't bothered to pin up the loose strands of hair that stuck to her neck. When I didn't respond, she leaned forward and rubbed my nose with hers.

"Things will be getting back to normal soon. I promise. But I mean it now. You can't be outside. Not tonight. Clara won't be here to tend to you either, but I trust that you'll be a big girl and obey. We'll all be back inside soon enough, and I'll read you a story before you go to bed. Does that sound good?"

"Yes, ma'am," I said, although I wasn't in the mood for a bedtime story.

"All right. I've got to go. Your papa needs me. You be good." She ruffled my hair before standing and leaving the room.

Her frantic dash down the stairs told me that the calm demeanor she'd pulled together in front of me was just an act for my sake.

Nobody had spoken to me in specific terms about what was happening. My age and the fact that I was a girl didn't warrant a sit-down explanation like my brothers, who were only a few years older, would get. Everyone had left me to my own deductions, perhaps thinking I was naive enough to skip and play through the storm in blissful ignorance. But I knew.

I'd heard the conversations between Mama and Papa behind the thin bedroom walls late at night when I was supposed to be sleeping. For what seemed like hours, they discussed their problems while I took it all in. One day when I was playing in the living room, Papa and Uncle Samuel fought in the kitchen about who had the greater authority to enforce discipline when Granddaddy was away on business. Because Papa was more gracious than Uncle Samuel, Granddaddy usually trusted him more with these matters. However, because of the severity of the situation, Uncle Samuel gathered enough men to support his opinion to get his way. The deal was done. Uncle Samuel got his victory.

I was only seven, but I absorbed it all and understood enough to know what the heightened flurry of activity was all about. Five nights before then, several slaves were caught trying to flee. This event piggybacked off the escape of four of our strongest men. That made things tough since it was the peak of the harvest season. Rumblings of another escape attempt were intercepted, so to end any future rebellion, my uncle changed the usual punishment from twenty lashes done in private to a public beating of double that amount. As Uncle Samuel put it, "We'll kill all six of them, if need be, to get it across that we're not putting up with this anymore. They need to be shown what they've got coming to 'em." He even ordered a special whip to be made. With Granddaddy being gone, no one was around to argue otherwise.

This event was a big deal for the community. Our neighbors came from miles around to show their support. More than anything, I think they came because they didn't want the same foolish ideas spreading to any of their slaves. Just their being there sent a clear, strong message to the lot of them. But I wasn't sure what that point was supposed to be. With Mama gone, I stood alone in my doubt.

The wisp of clouds grayed against the twilight. Their troubled frowns stretching across the sky made me anxious. Nature was tuned into something behind the scenes I couldn't hear, but the shiver it caused in my bones connected me to its unrest.

I picked up Otter, my stuffed bear, and held her close as I turned my attention to the window. I cautiously took a step closer and peeked at the scene below.

From the second-floor window, I had a view of the platform my brothers, Walter and Thomas, had helped finish earlier that afternoon. Each man had his own task, while Uncle Samuel had stood nearby with a watchful eye to make sure all the details were correct. Six posts, one for each perpetrator, were prepared. I'd watched the busyness from the kitchen while I helped Mama prepare the food. In and out the builders came all day, trailing their conversations behind them.

I waited till the door had just slammed behind the last man after the lunch break. "Do those slaves have families like us?" I'd asked Mama while whisking the eggs with the butter.

All I got was a stern look as she wiped down the kitchen counter. That wasn't the first time I'd bothered her with questions like that. I'd often seen the Negro children playing outside with their older siblings nearby and wanted to join them, but that was never allowed. One wave to them got me a quick slap on the hand. I learned my lesson.

Now in that final hour, their families were all I could think about. Clara, the woman who'd always taken care of me and who I'd known my whole life, was standing on the front row. Her son was one of the ones who'd been caught. She wept. Her head was raised to the heavens, and her lips moved with words I couldn't hear. I'd never before noticed the lines that bunched her eyes into a squint, because she'd always smiled. The sadness I sensed from her wrung out my feelings until a tear rimmed my eyes.

Tension reigned over the gathering crowd of

slaves. Most had been forced from their homes to come and watch. Children screamed. Parents patted their backs with no ease in the shrieks. Why would there have been? There was no comfort for the adults to give. A wet heat wrapped them in their misery that I felt through my own sweat and grief.

In contrast, some of our neighbors sat on blankets on the lawn, eating a late evening meal. Pastor Edmund played croquet with many of his parishioners on the grass. They all laughed and chatted as if they were on holiday. I watched the two different worlds until my eyes grew dry with the trying to understand.

There was one sermon in particular I remembered. It was the one when Pastor Edmund preached about love. I'm not sure why that one stood out to me—it wasn't because he magically talked any shorter—but he spoke about some man who was supposedly our neighbor being thrown into a ditch. He ended by saying that everyone is our neighbor and that we should love them like we love ourselves. The picture in the Bible, which gave me the real revelation, showed two men of different colors. One was lying on his back with his arm across his forehead in pain, while the other hovered over him as if he were taking care of him. I thought I finally understood something, until I tried to put it into practice when I asked if I could play with the slave children. That was when the truth was spanked slap out of me.

You would have thought that being white I would've had all the answers inserted into me at birth. I'd had lots of lessons about the origins of slavery. One day at recess, Molly gave me the best explanation I'd ever heard. Apparently, the slaves' evil was what made them so dark. She'd said that slavery was actually a blessing to those Africans because we saved them from their heathen culture. And now they owed us their loyalty because they would have died without us. Just to look at the likes of them, I guessed their sins must've been something horrible, considering how black it made their skin. Although I couldn't recall a specific time when any one of them had caused much trouble, until then.

I raised to my toes and strained to look closer. Something was happening. The neighbors put away their food and games and began to assemble around the platform. The chatter dropped to a hum all across both sides. That was when a line of heads came bobbing through the crowd, with my father and Uncle Samuel in the lead. When the four men and two women appeared and were led up the steps, I was instantly overwhelmed.

I closed my eyes, not in an intentional thought of prayer but to block out the paradox that played with my emotions. But in that vulnerable moment, I found myself praying to a God I thought existed only inside the four walls of the church.

"Dear God, please save the souls of those men and women. . . ." Those words came out naturally because I'd heard Mama recite that same prayer at least a dozen times. Then I added my own part. "I'm not exactly sure how this is supposed to work, but would you please help to bring us all together like that picture in the Bible? You know, the one where Jesus is hanging on the cross. Pastor Edmund said that's the greatest kind of love, although I don't really understand it. He said it was supposedly for everyone. If that's the case, then we need that kind of love. Um, amen."

When I opened my eyes, the wind picked up in a quick burst, crying through the cracks of the sill and vibrating the pane. It snaked around me and beat my heart at the same frantic pace it twirled the leaves in the tree next to the window. Its brisk sting awakened my senses to hope for something more.

I leaned forward, eager not to miss anything but too afraid to move my feet any closer. I squeezed Otter tighter to my chest.

My brothers had wanted to be on the platform and stand proud with my family. Mama had argued against it, saying she still wanted to preserve what was left of their innocence. But her weak dispute hadn't convinced Uncle Samuel otherwise. He was on a roll with his victories, and he made sure to gloat any chance he got.

"At thirteen and eleven, they're old enough

to learn the family business," he said and left Mama and me alone in the living room without her being able to say another word in defense. That was that, and Uncle Samuel was going to prove his authority to her.

"Walter, you take the lead," he said as he handed my oldest brother the chain on which all the slaves were attached. "Take them to their posts. That's a big job for a boy like you." Uncle Samuel patted Walter on his back.

Mama looked away as Walter obeyed. Pride crossed his face as the accused shuffled behind him. He positioned them in front of their posts. Walter and Thomas both helped to strap down the prisoners.

In a tinge of regret, I felt sorry for my brothers. I knew they were doing something wrong, although I couldn't put that thought into any kind of sensible words. It was just a sensation that ached in my heart.

Once everyone was secure, it was time for Papa to take charge. A hush followed his steps as he took longer, slower strides than normal to approach the center of the stage. His countenance demanded respect. His resolute actions sealed his authority. All eyes, including those from the smallest child, watched his final step as he turned to face the crowd.

I'd never seen Papa so menacing—he had to play the part given to him as the men of the plantation had to stand as a united front. At least that was the only way I justified his ruthless glare. I'd known Papa only from his hugs when he came in from work and when I sat on his lap as he read to me. Afraid of the conflicting sight, I hid slightly behind the sill, not daring to look at the fullness of the scene. I tried to catch my breath as I suddenly felt like an intruder in my own home. I continued to watch through the sheers that gently blew against my face, urging me to keep watching even when fear threatened to pull me away.

I plucked at the fur on top of Otter's head, one clump at a time, trying to soothe my rising panic.

When Uncle Samuel handed the list of the six ill-fated names to Papa, several moans rose from the family members. That unearthly noise muzzled the nervous chatter that had broken out. From my vantage point, I saw Clara collapse. I slapped my hand across my mouth to muffle the scream that came out. All I could do was helplessly watch as none of the other white people seemed to notice. However, those around her tended to her needs and comforted her. They quickly got her back on her feet.

Papa, in his stern appearance, seemed unfazed by the unfolding drama. He raised the list in front of him to read aloud their names and pronounce their sentence, but as he drew his breath, an unexpected figure emerged from the shadows. Gasps followed. Looking momentarily stunned, my father lowered the paper.

I moved closer and pressed my head against the screen for a better look. It was Kwame. The tips of my lashes brushed the screen as I blinked with anticipation, and in that brief moment, I forgot the gravity of the situation. I just wanted to hold on to the stalled second and make it count for even more.

When Kwame stepped into the fading light, his deformity seemed more pronounced than what the stories told about him. His mouth didn't close all the way, leaving his tongue to dangle partly out the side of it. Folds of skin buried his eyes, making them appear lopsided. His arms and legs hung in disproportionate lengths from his scrawny body. All he wore was an old pair of pants that must've been snatched off someone's line years before, and they were way too small for him.

Disfigured at birth, Kwame was deemed worthless by his own kind. His parents couldn't, or wouldn't, take care of him because they had to save their food rations for those who were fit. So, at the age of three, he was driven from the slave community and left to die.

"Savages," I'd heard Mama call his kind on multiple occasions, but we weren't any different. Even at my age, I knew full well—and I'm sure she did too—that we'd never extend our hand to help Kwame. And I was right.

The only smattering of compassion I ever saw was when I'd find Mama whispering prayers in the front pew for Kwame. She'd rock back and forth like she was in pain as she poured out the depths of her heart for him.

"Father, forgive the souls of the evil ones, for they know not what they do. Now in your loving arms, we commit Kwame to you. Please take him and save him."

I was never sure if she meant to save his soul like she always prayed for the other slaves so they wouldn't die heathens or to actually save him from the outside elements. Since she never really specified that detail in any of her prayers, I think God chose to take it upon himself to show us all what he could really do. Because, somehow, Kwame managed to survive on his own those eleven years as if God himself cradled him in his arms. And there he stood before us all without a worry of our disbelief.

All I could do was stare at the boy who'd defied all odds. Everyone else must've had the same sense of awe, because no one dared to make a sound. Or perhaps the tension was because Kwame's appearance created an uncomfortable homecoming. It was one thing for him to live on the outskirts of our stories. It was quite another for him to actually show up and enter back into our lives.

Papa stared at Kwame in silence, as if trying to decide what to do with the interruption that had completely disrupted the momentum. It was even more unbelievable that not even Uncle Samuel had anything to say. His mouth was drawn tight as if analyzing how best to use that situation to his advantage. He just hadn't come up with anything yet.

Chandler, the mule, was the only one bold enough to snort his loud opinion in the tension of the moment. He'd moseyed up to the fence, unnoticed in all the fuss. Kwame took that whinnying grunt as his cue to move.

With all eyes on him, he waddled his way to the platform with unbalanced steps. Whispers broke out across the crowd. Kwame's head jiggled to the left and right as he greeted everyone in a spastic nod and wave. His smile portrayed an ecstatic joy like he was just returning from a short trip he'd had with friends.

When he got closer to Papa, Kwame shouted, "Me," while beating his chest with flailing hands. As Kwame awkwardly swung himself up onto the platform, Papa took a step back to give him room to roll onto the platform.

That was when the man at the end of the row shouted, "Kwame?"

The boy turned his attention to the man. Then Kwame half-stumbled, half-loped his way down to greet him.

"Papa! Mama!" Kwame said, stomping his feet with delight.

The woman next to him sobbed even louder. The sound raised the hair on my arms. I hadn't realized that two of the captured escapees were Kwame's parents. I leaned closer to catch every word. Everyone else did the same.

"Boy, you can't be here," his father said. "Go on now. This business doesn't concern you."

Kwame simply turned back around and shuffled away. It was like he was on a mission he'd already mapped out.

"Me. I take. I take it for them," Kwame said as he approached Papa and snatched the whip from his hand without any fear of unwritten rules. "Let me take." He swatted his body in a frantic demonstration.

Papa remained stoic as confusion rattled the crowd. The prisoners seemed just as baffled. The man in the middle took the opportunity to try to squirm his way out of the chains, but Uncle Samuel had finally recovered.

"You take?" Uncle Samuel asked Kwame, yelling above the crowd to regain their attention.

Everyone settled back down.

Uncle Samuel kicked the ankles of the man trying to escape as he walked by. His sheer meanness gave him an added girth to be reckoned with. Many men overshadowed him in size but never attempted to defeat him. Uncle Samuel focused his anger on Kwame and grabbed his arm. He loved to perform a good show.

Kwame vigorously nodded and didn't try to shake loose from his grip.

"Yes. I take," he said.

"What did you take, boy?" Uncle Samuel threw Kwame's arm back down and shoved him back. "Did you steal something? If you did, you'll have to wait your turn. I won't have any problem tending to you next."

"I take. Me." Kwame patted his chest, and then pointed to the prisoners. "I take their place. For them. Me."

His continued hand motions indicated what people had already guessed. People shook their heads, and even his own kind shooed him away out of what seemed like sheer embarrassment for him. But Kwame stayed put. He wanted Papa to release the prisoners while he took their punishment.

I didn't know numbness could feel so frigid as it seized my body in a state of horror. It shook me enough to stay focused.

Even if Papa felt that this was the most ridiculous thing he'd ever heard, he didn't show it. "Go on now, Kwame," he said. His tone found pity for him. "Like your father said, this doesn't concern you."

Papa grasped Kwame's elbow to lead him out of harm's way, but the boy wouldn't budge.

Kwame was a year older than Walter, but he looked much smaller because of years of malnourishment. However, with his determination, it would've taken an army of men to usher him off that platform.

"I've had enough," said Uncle Samuel, clenching his hands into fists. He put his nose to within inches of Kwame. "If you're so eager, how about you go first? Then we can go about our business."

The white men snickered and offered agreements.

"I go first." Kwame nodded and jammed and twisted the whip into Uncle Samuel's closed fists. He lumbered to the nearest woman and patted her back. "First. Her. I take her place."

Wide-eyed, the woman didn't flinch. She stared straight at the post in front of her.

Uncle Samuel stood silent, rubbed his chin, and then, acting like a shrewd businessman, took Kwame up on the offer.

"Okay, Kwame, just as long as someone is punished for her crime, you may take her place. Are you sure that's what you want?"

Many gasped in disbelief, including Papa. Kwame's fumbling fingers were already trying to release the woman.

Amid the clamoring chains, the woman looked past Kwame and asked, "Why are you doing this?" Her faltering whisper was laced with fear.

Kwame gently patted her head. "I love you."

Papa advanced toward Uncle Samuel to call a meeting, but my uncle raised his hand to stop him. His face was red, like he'd had enough.

"Go help Kwame get her down," he ordered. "Then we'll get on with it."

The expression on Papa's face told his displeasure, but he followed orders. He couldn't appear weak in front of the crowd. When the woman was freed, cheers rose from her family and outstretched arms helped her off the platform. At that moment, I'm certain no one else cared that Kwame was about to be flogged. His own strapping to the post went unnoticed, except by me.

My stare produced a tear that burnt my face with its sting, and I used Otter's whole body to wipe it off my cheek.

Kwame's face was peaceful, despite the fact that his arms were contorted above his head and his body was sprawled unmercifully across the boards. The crowd wasn't even paying him any attention.

I didn't understand what was happening, why no one seemed to care. I clenched my teeth in an anger I didn't even know I had.

Uncle Samuel was ready for this to be over and didn't wait for any more distractions. When he raised the whip, the curtains sucked against my cheek while the earth paid its reverence in the form of a quieted awe.

Then it happened.

The whip, braided with shards of glass, snapped across Kwame's back. But as his face distorted in agony, neither cursing nor pain did he utter. Instead, a song purer than the spring rains rose from his cavernous depths in the form of a simple prayer—"Lord, love them, love them, as you love me. Use me, Lord, to set them free."

The first note, surprising in its strength, crushed the commotion. All conversations immediately ceased. No one expected a powerful voice from such a small boy. He had the attention of every living creature, human or not. The mule stopped mid-chew to stare. The youngest child quieted his sniffles to take notice. Even the world paused in its responsibilities of humming bees and murmuring flies to pay homage to the song. Kwame sang for those who'd shunned him, for those who punished him, and for those who didn't care.

Uncle Samuel paused only momentarily, then got back to work. All the while, Kwame's song continued through each debilitating strike.

Staggering, swaying currents reached my hiding place. Maybe I was too weak, or its power too strong, but it beckoned my soul to bathe in its liberty. I gave in to the melody as it rose with every treble and dimmed with every bass, giving life to my floundering heart. It invited me to stay within its depths, and I begged to learn more.

God answered my unconscious prayer as nature responded where man failed to understand. The pond donned haze in a mournful mask. Passing clouds shrouded the emerging stars. All the landscape grieved in black, except for the ground that claimed his blood. The red drops trickled into a pool below, while the dirt cupped its hands around it in an act of respect.

When the world seemed bound in an irrevocable trance, the last strike resounded, silencing the remaining words with its thundering clap.

All grew unnervingly still. In my weakened yet euphoric state, I dropped Otter to the ground.

When Kwame was released, he fell, trembling, to his hands and knees. Uncle Samuel wiped spattered blood from his forehead and cheeks with his sleeve. In that quiet moment, before Kwame could move, a restless murmur stirred the crowd. I knew they wanted more. I desired it too—not to see the painful blows that struck Kwame's body but to be lured back into the shelter of his song that allowed the soul to drink a peace that was foreign to hostile man and woman.

Mama darted from her place in the background to help Kwame, but Uncle Samuel quickly moved to stand in her way. The look on her face told me that she'd had enough of Uncle Samuel's bullying. With gritted teeth, she beat his chest and screamed at him until he finally gave into her incessant demand. He scowled but stepped out of the way.

Curious by her compassion, everyone watched in silence as she knelt to meet Kwame. He lifted up ever so slightly as she wrapped a towel around him and cleaned him off. She shook with a tremor I'd only seen through her prayers.

"All right, Kwame," Papa said, not looking at Uncle Samuel. "You can go."

"No," he said, barely able to shake his head.

Five more prisoners awaited their fate. Kwame was determined to continue. Mama backed away to give him space as he crawled to the next post. Our gaze was transfixed on his slow progression, and the distant chug and swoosh from the old gristmill paced his painful movement.

When Kwame reached the next man, he pointed at him and said, "Again." Blood trickled from his mouth, and he slurped it up as best he could.

"Kwame," Papa spoke softly and knelt beside him. This was more the father I knew.

"Again!" Kwame interrupted, banging the platform with the palm of his hand. His head drooped as he sucked in a deep, shuddering breath. "I take it for them," he said, exhaling into a trembling posture that rattled the loose board beneath him.

Papa took a long pause before looking at Uncle Samuel. My uncle nodded his permission. Papa stood, and as he backed away, he averted his eyes to the ground. He didn't look as though he wanted Kwame's beatings to continue but had no other choice. What was he going to do? Even Kwame wanted to continue.

When Walter unfettered the second prisoner, only a few people stirred. All were focused on this once rejected boy, who painted a picture of a love so profound it reached past the limits of man.

Uncle Samuel again raised the whip, and when the first strike snapped across Kwame's back, strength like a healing balm renewed his voice. He sang over and over again, as loud as he could, "Lord, love them, love them, as you love me. Use me, Lord, to set them free."

Slap and crack, slap and crack, the whip drew out a song that stripped away layers of lies. I closed my eyes, too fearful to watch, yet I yearned to remain in the song's spell. Kwame sang for my heart, he sang for my soul, and he sang for my quivering core. As the chorus tenderly advanced to challenge my doubt, my tears gave way and released in a torrential pour. I knew what was happening, what prayer had dared to come true. In the form of a boy, all those pictures I'd known became a living piece of art that destroyed the boundaries of man.

When the song ended, I opened my eyes to face the ugliness of reality. I didn't want to see Kwame's blood, the gouges in his skin, or his protruding bones, but I made myself look at the cost that was paid for my uncertainty. That shock of conviction left me standing whole.

And Kwame's work was still not done. Two more times he acted with the same moving results. By this time, no one cheered when the prisoners were released nor did they move at the final note. The tension laced a string around us that pulled us together as one. With our hearts beating in unity, we all knew what was yet to come.

With only two more left, barely able to move, Kwame dragged himself to his mother. The crowd stood motionless. We watched. We waited. With his body sprawled on the ground, Kwame tried four times before he could lift his finger and point. No words could he speak.

My sobs waned with the tension.

Finally, when it seemed as if Kwame had nothing left to give, he said, "Mama, I do this for you."

I'll never forget that unearthly wail that came from a mama's broken heart. It sounded like a thousand banshees being skinned alive. She shook her head and flounced about with the chains rattling their fury against the post. "No, Kwame, no!" She screamed. "Not for me! I don't deserve it."

Kwame couldn't move to comfort her. He rolled his head over so that his eyes could meet hers.

By that time my own mama had completely lost her composure. She buried her head in the blood-stained towel and wept.

Kwame's father shook his head. With tears streaming down his face, he said, "Kwame, you can't take any more. Let us bear this punishment, not you." His eyes darted to Uncle Samuel as he pled. "Don't let him do it. It's my fault. I did it. I'll take my own punishment."

Before my uncle could answer, Kwame said, "No, I do this for you. That's why I'm here. I came back for you."

Kwame was too weak to even raise his head to look at my uncle, but that didn't stop him from saying, "Let them go."

Though Uncle Samuel hesitated, he honored Kwame's request. When he asked my brothers to release both of Kwame's parents, he was shaking. I wondered what was going on inside his head. I'd never seen Uncle Samuel look weak in the presence of a slave.

At that time, neither Kwame's mama nor his daddy moved from his side. They stood by him while he was secured into place. His father wrapped his hands around Kwame's and held them tight. Then he lowered his head and wept until the other men had to yank him back. His father fell backward but wouldn't leave the platform.

Then it was the last time. Uncle Samuel barely swung the whip. Although he took easier swings, Kwame's back and sides were so raw he had to twist his body, allowing his chest to take the brunt. In the midst of it all, his voice stayed strong to lift us up in prayer.

"Lord, love them, love them, as you love me. Use me, Lord, to set them free."

The creek muted its chatter. The birds ceased their flight. I pressed the palms of my hands against the glass, trying to absorb it all and hold it in. And as the final note held suspended, the air became saturated with its richness until it broke loose in a torrent of lament. A choir of bullfrogs joined the dying anthem in a fury of protest. The strength of the pines shuddered in its wake. The wind howled in dispute and scattered the crepe myrtle blossoms with its tantrum, and silence— as a welcomed breath—stole past the anguishing cries with a calm so taut, all gave it respect.

Kwame was sustained until the very last.

When Uncle Samuel eased him from his perch, Kwame had nothing left to give. He collapsed into his mother's waiting arms and gave his final breath.

I clutched my chest, feeling a deep sense of loss. My fingers, moist with sweat, lowered the window into place. I didn't want to hear any more. Silence rang in my ears as I backed against the wall and slid down until my knees covered my face. I felt changed, but I didn't know how to describe what I'd witnessed.

Not long after Kwame died, the place where he'd been living was discovered. He'd dug out a hole beneath the foundation of the abandoned barn that sat by the river. A nest of old clothes made the bed. Scattered bones of birds, rabbits, and squirrels showed his survival skills. And all those pictures he'd torn from the Bible were placed around the living area under rocks. The well-worn picture next to the bed was the one of Jesus hanging on the cross.

As a child that picture had never been my favorite. I preferred the ones where David was slaying Goliath or Jesus was laughing with the children. Those I understood. When we sang, "Jesus loves me—this I know, for the Bible tells me so," it was easier to imagine Jesus smiling at me while I sat comfortably in his lap than to think of him dying on the cross.

But Kwame taught me something different. He sang with words of conviction, "Lord, love them, love them, as you love me. Use me, Lord, to set them free." He was moved into action because of his love for us, and it certainly had nothing to do with the fact than anyone loved him first. No one did—no one but God. Kwame was rejected for his inabilities, but he didn't condemn us. He was ridiculed because of his behavior, but he respected us. He was left to be forgotten, but he came back for us. He demonstrated a love that cost him everything—the same love that Jesus displayed. Though we had the teaching and the knowledge that went with that picture of Jesus, Kwame understood it better than the rest of us. It was like God poured unmerited wisdom into the most unlikely person and kept him alive until that very day just for us. And Kwame didn't even live to see the effect his love had on us.

That night we came together as one people. No more beatings took place. No longer did we judge each other by the color of skin. All of us worshiped God together under the same roof. Not long after that day, the war broke out, and our family and neighbors fought for the other side, for the freedom of our brothers and sisters of different colors. We lived out a love that cost us everything—our plantations, many lives in the war, respect from those who didn't understand— but we gained so much more from the heart of an unwanted slave. He had lived out the picture of true love—and it liberated us all.

CHAPTER 8

Freedom's Song

♫

I've forgotten my home. Lush hills and green valleys are now make-believe thoughts locked in distant memories. My calloused hands toil this dusty ground, aching for a taste of that freedom. Is this slavery? Nah, it's just life—the all-work, no-play grind of another day gone by. But every once in a while, when all's quiet in the field, I hear those hills a-calling. Their sweet whispers of hope penetrate this doubting heart of mine and ignite a passion to keep the memory of where I came from alive.

I look into the eyes of li'l children born under this darkened yoke. The only light they know is the sun, which means hard labor, scorched necks, and thirsting souls. And that ain't hope. My mama once said that drawing a picture with color would open the eyes of a blind man; painting a picture with words would open the ears of the deaf. With this power, someone could make these children taste a whole other world and bring it within their reach. So that's just what I did.

Mama Tabs is what all the li'l children called me. "Tell us another story, Mama Tabs," they'd say. So in the fields all blown with cotton, my stories began. Some were funny; some were downright silly. But my favorite was the story about a li'l lost lightning bug. Who knew such a small creature could bring us hope? But it did. All would work and listen 'til the only sound heard was its voice among the swish, whish of pulled cotton. And this is how my story began . . .

In the starlit fields a glow swooped, looped past yellow daisies dimmed by the night, fumbling, bumbling beyond the shadows fading 'til morning light. The lightning bug flickered on, then ran to hide, waking the world from slumber with a twinkle of hope against the darkened sky. A hum, a song, a melody played upon her wings: "Freedom, freedom is in me to soar the waves that breezes bring, to spread my light to every part and sing the song that fills my heart." When the day shone bright, her job was done, and she rested until the falling sun.

All was well in the long summer days, but then they began to wane, and an autumn wind blew from the west and chilled the landscape's veins. The drowsy bug, with no hint of change, awakened to the wind and reeled in fright when a gust so grand grabbed her from her den. It threw her, bumbling, bobbling over hills and towns, and she soared without a flutter. Flipping, flopping, she found her wings, but they began to stutter. "Help me . . . free me. Oh, hapless wind. Where is it you take me? To far off lands? Past the seas? To where I've never been?" A sad melody ensued. And when she stopped, the land was gray. It was a dark and foreign land.

Tears fell—vast and wide. They washed the barren ground. And through the blur, a figure stood. Solemn. Bleak. Forlorn.

"Help me," the li'l bug cried. Her voice cracked. Her wings drooped.

But the figure only moaned, "Help you? A little bug? That I cannot do." Off the figure marched, leaving the bug behind. Despair and fear quenched freedom's song, and a hope that had once taken flight left her grounded, her soul depleted.

The li'l bug drew her wings in close. They were no longer used for soaring. She slumped against the biting wind. The darkness overtook her. She walked on her tiny legs and dodged the cracks of broken land. In her defeat, she gave up hope. She was lost and all alone. This was a far and desolate land, a land that was not her own.

Then the pitter of li'l feet rushed at her from behind. A hand swooped down and picked her up, and a li'l girl's voice chimed, "Your light, your light, I saw your light. It twinkled through the shadows, casting out the night."

Shocked, the li'l bug looked back to see what had caused the fuss. She realized in her pity and in her shame, she'd forgotten who she was. With a light of sparkling splendor and wings crafted to set her free, she was the lightning bug, a hope bug that brings light so all can see. She felt pride surge through her, and her feet lifted from the ground. Her wings spread wide and caught the currents in this new freedom she had found. In a flutter, in a float, she dove and climbed while her wings hummed in victory, "Freedom, freedom within me as I soar upon the wind to far off lands and past these seas where my heart has been. Though the winds may blow me hither, it cannot take my song. It is freedom, freedom in me, that carries me along."

Her li'l light grew in strength and pierced the hold of night. The girl danced barefoot to the carefree ditty while the birds all took to flight. The hills were bathed in greens, yellows, and blues, while the lilies arose to the clamor. The streams all awoke with babbling prose, and the trees shook and shimmered. It was still the same land, a far-off land, a land that was not her home, but it came alive with a forgotten pulse wherever she did roam. Her song was heard throughout the valleys and where every beast did stand:

"Though darkness threatens to overtake me, I must remember who I am. With wings to soar and a light to shine, this is how I'm made. It is freedom, freedom in me, and you can't take that away."

When my story is done, I can hear the li'l children's thoughts among the methodical rhythm of their hands. And though they live in a world that is not their home, they know of their own light deep down inside them. It is suppressed and forgotten and longs to shine. It's their freedom, theirs alone to have, while a whole other world that this darkness can't steal from them waits within their reach.

As I look toward the heavens, I give a smile and hear those sweet hills a-calling. I live in a world, a world not my home, but I'll let my light shine through. And I'll tell you a secret no one else knows: that li'l lightning bug is me.

CHAPTER 9

Out of the Author's Journal

Part 3

♫

The world knows ugly, even in what can seem like the most idealistic of situations. Many try to cover up the mess in their lives with a mirage of beauty. We want it, seek it, and grab after things that mimic it, but we are ultimately left with a forgery that erodes with time. The good news is that there really is true beauty out there, even in the pain.

Grace, love, redemption, purpose—these are just a few examples of the beauty found only in a holy God who desires a relationship with his creation again. Sin broke our relationship with our Creator, and there's nothing we can do on our own to mend it. In fact, if left to our own design, we don't want God to interfere in our lives at all. Sin has diluted that desire to hope for something more, but God never wanted to leave that distance between us. Through his plan of restoration, he sent his Son, Jesus, as the perfect sacrifice for our sins to die on the cross in order for that relationship to be restored. Through that selfless act God tirelessly, consistently, and endlessly pursues us with his love, even when we keep turning our backs on him.However, this isn't the story of God that is necessarily heard. With the world being flipped upside down because of sin, the image of a loving God is often missed, and his beauty is distorted by all the noise. Instead, he's often viewed as being distant, uncaring, and even unloving. Others don't even want to believe there's a God at all, because what they see and experience has left them empty. However, the actions of my characters reflect a beauty that's already there, waiting to be discovered. That's why I write. I want to show people that there really is something more. The beauty of God can be found in the unexplainable love and actions of others.

I've discovered that truth. Underneath the static of all the noise, there's a song. It's a love song sung by our Creator God, who's luring you and me back to him. And that's the heartbeat of my stories.